THE EVERLASTING NOW

THE EVERLASTING NOW

Sara Harrell Banks

PEACHTREE
ATLANTA

Published by
PEACHTREE PUBLISHERS
1700 Chattahoochee Avenue
Atlanta, Georgia 30318-2112
www.peachtree-online.com

Cover design by Loraine M. Joyner
Book design and composition by Melanie McMahon Ives

Manufactured in the United States of America
10 9 8 7 6 5 4 3 2 1
First Edition

Library of Congress Cataloging-in-Publication Data
Banks, Sara H., 1942–
  The Everlasting Now / written by Sara Harrell Banks.
    p. cm.
  Summary: In 1937 Alabama, eleven-year-old Brother helps with his mother's boardinghouse, gains insight into prejudice when he befriends the nephew of the family's maid, and dreams of riding a train one day with the railroad men who serve as his substitute fathers.
  ISBN 978-1-56145-525-6 / 1-56145-525-3
  [1. Boardinghouses—Fiction. 2. Depressions—1929—Fiction. 3. Friendship—Fiction. 4. Race relations—Fiction. 5. Family life—Alabama—Fiction. 6. Alabama—History—20th century—Fiction.] I. Title.
  PZ7.B22635Ch 2010
  [Fic]—dc22
                                2009024512

For my brother Mike Harrell
and in loving memory of our stepfather
Edward L. Cooper,
engineer, Central of Georgia Railroad
                                    —S. H. B.

Chapter One

When I first met Champion Luckey, I didn't know that he was going to change my life. Maybe you never know when that's going to happen; it's not like something you're expecting. It's more like getting struck by lightning and living to tell about it.

'Course he was the one who got struck first and I did it, but I didn't mean to.

The reason I met him in the first place was because of his aunt, Lily Luther. She's the cook at our boardinghouse, and pretty much runs everything, including me.

One day, I asked Mama if we paid Lily.

"Of course," she said.

"Not enough," said Lily from the kitchen.

"Well, if she works for us," I whispered, "how come she's the boss of everything?"

"Because she's better at it than I am," said Mama.

* * *

On the first day of summer vacation, I slept late, then went downstairs for breakfast. Lily was standing at the Roper stove stirring a pot of black-eyed peas and listening to Sugar Blues on the radio, her skinny body swaying in time to the music.

"'Bout time you showed up, Brother," she said. "I need you to go to the dairy for buttermilk. The railroad men'll be here directly, and they'll be expectin' my biscuits."

I picked up a piece of toast and started buttering it. "Can't I eat breakfast first?"

Lily watched me with her hawk eyes. Her skin's the color of sourwood honey—not brown and not black. She wore a white flower behind one ear. "That's enough butter," she said.

"This toast is cold, it needs more."

"Brother Sayre, put the buttered sides against your tongue. It'll taste fine. If you'd come to breakfast when you're supposed to, instead of polin' around wastin' time, it wouldn't be cold. Hurry up, now. Get two jars of jelly from the pantry—scuppernong, the kind Mr. Holman likes."

That meant that I was to go swap something for something else. This time we were gonna swap jelly for buttermilk at Mr. Holman's dairy. Swapping stuff was a big thing in Snow Hill, Alabama, in 1937. We were in the Great Depression, although there was nothing great about it. Songs were written about it and how everybody was suffering.

2

The Everlasting Now

Mama's always singing about hard times, railroads, and lonesome valleys. Lily just sings the blues.

* * *

Seems like hard times happened to everybody. The stock market crashed, so a lot of people lost all their money; then there was a run on the banks and folks that had money took it out of the banks. A terrible dust storm in Oklahoma and Kansas ruined the crops in the fields, so farmers had to leave their farms and go to California to find work. Some did, some didn't.

Here in Snow Hill, the Mercantile Bank closed, the shirt factory shut down, men got laid off at the sawmill, and some stores had to close 'cause there wasn't any business. About the only real business that was still working was the railroad.

My daddy was the editor and publisher of the town's only newspaper, the *Choctaw Herald*. And it had to shut down. He explained that since folks couldn't afford to advertise in the paper, he couldn't afford to print it. He also said that a town without a newspaper was a poor town, indeed. After he closed the newspaper office, he left home to look for work. And that's when the worst thing of all happened to our family.

Daddy went to North Carolina to apply for a job at a big paper. But when he got there, the people who worked for the paper—the journalists, reporters, and linotype operators— went on strike against the paper. Well, being a newspaper man, Daddy couldn't cross the picket lines. Then, delivery trucks rolled up and instead of picking up papers, men got out of the trucks and started beating the strikers. That's when Daddy got killed. He was just trying to help, but I guess they got him mixed up with the strikers and somebody hit him in the head with a tire iron. That was two years ago. We all miss him something awful.

My mama, my sister Swan, and I live in Grandpapa Yeatman's big old house that he'd left to Mama when he died. Because of the Depression, we didn't have much money, and there weren't many jobs in Snow Hill.

"But we have to make a living," said Mama. "Only I can't get a job around here. It's hard enough for men to find jobs. Besides, I don't know how to do anything but keep house."

"You can do lots of things," I said. "You're a good reader and a pretty good cook, and you grow stuff too."

"Nothing I could get paid for," she said, "but thank you anyway. We'll think of something."

She started walking through the house like she was looking for something. I followed her upstairs. She went into each of the five bedrooms and even into the trunk room that belongs to my little sister. Then we went through all the rooms downstairs. And when she finished the tour, Mama stood there looking up at the picture of Grandpapa Yeatman in his black judge's robe hanging over the mantle. "Your grandpapa left me this house to do with as I please," she told me. "And he'd have wanted us to survive these hard times. In fact, he'd have *expected* us to survive."

The Everlasting Now

So she decided to open a boardinghouse for nice people.

Some people in town didn't think she should, since she was the judge's daughter and it didn't look proper. They acted like it was *their* house, instead of ours. But Mama paid them no mind, she just went about her business. And that's when Lily came to work for us and started to run our lives.

* * *

Lily took the pot of peas off the stove and, putting her hands on her hips, gave me her hawk look.

"Brother Sayre," she said, "stop daydreamin' and get about your business."

A railroad calendar hung on the inside of the pantry door. On it was a picture of *The Twentieth Century Limited*, the most beautiful steam engine in the world, rounding a curve of track like she's riding to glory. Mr. Edwards, who's one of our boarders and a railroad engineer, had given it to me.

Homemade jellies, preserves, fruits, and vegetables lined the shelves from top to bottom. We grew most of what we ate. Every season, Mama and Lily put up peaches, tomatoes, applesauce, beans, watermelon pickles, and just about anything else that grew in the garden. I took down two jars of golden scuppernong jelly and patted the calendar on my way out.

"Lily," I said, putting the jelly jars into a paper sack, "reckon how long this Depression's gonna last?"

"Don't be asking me about the Depression," she said. "It don't mean much to *me*. Don't mean much to any Negroes. We was born in depression. It only became official when it hit the whites. Now, before you go, run on and see does your mama want anything from town."

I went upstairs to the sewing room. I heard Mama before I saw her. She was singing about trains, keeping time with her foot on the treadle of the sewing machine. "*This* train is bound for glory, this train…" *Thump… thump…thump…*

Mama was mending sheets. She'd split them down the middle where they were worn, turn the outside edges to the inside, then make a new seam. Keeping a boardinghouse takes a lot of sheets.

She looked up when I came in. She was wearing one of Daddy's old shirts and trousers rolled at the ankles. Her curly brown hair was piled on top of her head.

"Lily says do you need anything from town?"

"Just the mail," she said. "And I'd like for you to stop by the library. Miss Eulalie has a book for me."

Downstairs, in the shadowy hall, a man's hat hung on the hall tree. It's my daddy's best hat, a dark brown Dunlop felt with a kind of silky hatband. After his funeral, the preacher said I'd have to be the man of the house. That was a joke. I was only ten when Daddy died. But that's when I claimed the hat for my own. It was too big, but I started wearing it anyway, hoping it'd make me look older.

I'm almost twelve now, and I still don't look like the man of any house. I'm skinny, there's a gap between my front teeth, and my hair flops down over my forehead like I'm wearing bangs. I looked in the mirror, tilted the hat the way Daddy had worn it, and went out the front door.

My sister Swan, who's eight, was sitting in the wooden swing with her cat, Shirley Boligee, a calico with white fur and splotches the color of orange marmalade.

Twisting a strand of her blonde curly hair, Swan looked up from reading *Mary Poppins*. The bridge of her nose was peppered with freckles.

"Where you goin'?"

"To town, then the dairy," I said.

"Can I go?"

"No. It's too far and you'd whine all the way home."

"Then bring me back a Goo Goo Cluster," she said, batting her eyelashes like she always does when she wants something.

"I don't have a nickel for candy," I said. "I don't even have a nickel."

* * *

Our house is on Old Post Road, about where town ends and country begins. There's a white wooden fence around the property. A gravel drive leading up to the side of the house has a cattle gap at the end that makes a rolling sound like thunder when somebody drives over it. I walked down to the front gate and saw that somebody had drawn another picture of a cat on one of the fence posts. It's a hobo sign that means "a kindhearted woman lives here."

There's lots of folks wandering around because they don't have any homes on account of the Depression. Hobos find us because of the marks on the fence posts. Mama said they're secret maps showing where they can find a meal or work. Sometimes Lily threatens to scrub off the signs.

"Those folks are gon' eat us out of house and home," she said. But the marks stay and the hungry get fed.

Chapter Two

The marble floor of the post office was cool under my bare feet. Mr. Bartram, the postmaster, stood at the brass-grilled window, his green eyeshade reflecting the slow-turning ceiling fan. He was looking over at the mural painted on the opposite wall. Field hands were working the cotton fields, picking the bolls and putting them in bags slung over their shoulders. They were all smiling to beat the band. But there's nothing to smile about. Picking cotton is just hard work. A lot of it goes on around here.

"That Federal Arts Project, the FAP, that the gov'ment runs is a good thing, I reckon," he said. "It puts artists to work and all, but the fella painted that one sure didn't know 'bout cotton."

As he handed me the mail, Miz Edna Earl crossed the lobby, the heels of her shoes clicking like castanets on the marble floor...*tippy tap...tippy tap...tippy tap*. She was short and plump, and when she walked, she tilted from side to side, like her girdle was too tight.

"Mornin', Mr. Bartram," she said. She gave me a hard look. "You're supposed to take your hat off in the presence of a lady, Brother."

I took it off 'cause I didn't want to have to explain my daddy's hat to her, again.

Miz Edna Earl rented out rooms, too, but was too stingy to give her boarders a decent meal. Nobody stayed with her unless they were lost or flat-out desperate. She couldn't stand it that our boarders worked for the Southern Railroad and could pay board. And not only that, everybody in town respected railroad men. And the engineer, Mr. Edwards, was treated like a real important person, which he is.

"Are y'all having problems with hobos out your way, Brother?" Miz Edna Earl asked. "They surely are a problem in town. There's no excuse for begging, in my opinion." She acted like she'd never heard of the Depression.

"They come by from time to time," I said, backing toward the door. For sure, nobody'd ever draw a cat figure on her fence posts.

When I got outside, I put my hat back on and took a deep breath; the air smelled of dust, honeysuckle, and oak leaves. I walked around the corner to the library, a small white house only two rooms deep. The uneven, splintery floors creaked under my feet as I went inside. Nobody was there except the librarian. I took off my hat and went over to the desk. A vase of pink and white roses smelled sweet in the warm room.

Miss Eulalie peered at me over her glasses. "Good to see

you, Brother," she said, picking up a book and removing the note tucked in it.

"I have *The Good Earth,* by Pearl S. Buck, for your mama." She always said the author's name along with the title. While she checked it out, I went over to the shelves and picked out *Wild Horse Mesa.* Mr. Edwards had got me started on Zane Grey's books. I liked them a lot. I told Miss Eulalie goodbye and put my hat back on. Just as I stepped onto the porch, the sheriff came out of the jailhouse across the street.

Sheriff Montrose "Piggy" Hamm was in full uniform, with hobnail boots, a pistol, bullets on a belt around his fat belly, and a mean-looking blackjack in his back pocket.

I was afraid of him. He hadn't ever done anything to me, but he looked like he wanted to. Once I found a dead bird in the woods; maggots were crawling over it. It made me sick and I threw up in the bushes. I didn't tell 'cause I didn't want anybody to think I'm a sissy. But that's how the sheriff made me feel.

He watched me from across the street. As I reached the bottom step, he quick slapped his hands against his sides and stared straight at me. Slowly, he raised his right hand like it was a pistol. With his other hand, he pulled his thumb back like he was cocking it. Then, aiming the make-believe gun at me, he pulled the trigger.

"Bang!" he said, grinning like a mule eating briars.

He thinks he's funny, but he's not. He's just a big bully. Mama said she couldn't understand how he got the job in the first place. He'd come to Snow Hill from some other town after he'd been fired. But the mayor hired him anyway.

I walked away like I didn't even see him, paying him no mind. But I was sure glad when I turned the corner and was out of his sight. I hightailed it out of there, fast as I could.

On the dusty road to the dairy, my feet were soon covered in red clay dust. My overalls were sticking to my back, and I was sweating under Daddy's hat. Clouds of midges rose up from the grass like tiny, buggy tornadoes, and the sack of jelly jars, mail, and books felt heavier and heavier.

Down the road, a bicycle rider wobbled in and out of patches of shade. A long stick stuck straight out from one side of his bike. A minute later, he wheeled up to me in a cloud of dust.

Lucius Polite was a tall, skinny man with only one leg; the other got cut off on the railroad tracks a long time ago. He balanced his bicycle by using his crutch on the same side as his one leg.

"Whuh's Mr. Saywa?" said Lucius, puffing the words out like he was blowing out a candle. He couldn't pronounce the letter *r*.

"He's gone, Lucius," I said. I'd told him a hundred times my daddy was dead, but he always asked about him.

"I'm sowwy," he said.

Years ago, Daddy bought Lucius a bicycle and taught him to ride it. Lucius never forgot him. I guess he hadn't known many kindnesses in his life.

He rubbed at his hair, which was full of leaves and twigs.

"I need me a hat," he said. He seemed to be admiring mine, but since his left eye wandered, it was hard to tell. Some folks said Lucius had second sight on account of his funny eye; they thought he could see into the future. He'd never predicted anything except rain, as far as I know.

"Maybe I can find one for you at home," I said, "but I'm not making a promise."

Lucius smiled, then rode off to parts unknown. He didn't have a home; sometimes he slept in a boxcar on a railroad siding, other times he stayed in a shed somewhere in the woods. That could account for the state of his hair. A hat might help, I thought.

* * *

The air felt cooler in the deep shade of the pecan grove as I went up the narrow road to Holmans' dairy. The house was white, with wide porches. It sat back from the road in a grove of pecan trees. In the fall, Mr. and Mrs. Holman sold pecans as well as milk and butter. There was a big gray barn out back. Down in the pasture, cows stood rump high in the pond, trying to stay cool.

I walked around to the back and knocked on the screened door. Mrs. Holman came out, wiping her hands on her apron.

"Well, hey, Brother," she said. "Good to see you. How's your mama? I don't get to see Miss Serena very often. I know she's busy. Is your sister okay? She's such a pretty little thing."

"They're fine," I said, handing her the jars of golden jelly. "It's scuppernong."

"That's Lonnie's favorite. Now, before you go, he says for you to come out to the barn. There's something he wants you to see." She shuddered slightly. "I'll leave your buttermilk here in the shade of the porch."

The barn smelled of hay, cows, and fertilizer. Dust motes drifted in the sunlight shining through the wide board walls. Mr. Holman was mucking out the stalls.

"Come on in, Brother!" he called. "I want to show you something."

I could see why Mrs. Holman had shuddered. Curled up in a flat bushel basket, and deader than a doornail, was a six-foot rattler as big around as a man's wrist.

"Holy cow!" I said, stepping back a tad. "That's the biggest snake I ever saw!" I was impressed, but I didn't want to get too close. I don't like snakes, dead or alive.

"It's somethin', isn't it?" he said, settling his cap on the back of his head. "Dogs were havin' a fit out back, and when I went to take a look, that's what I found, so I shot it. After dinner, I'm takin' it down to Mr. Harper's store to show everybody."

* * *

When I got home, Lily was shucking corn at the kitchen table. I put the milk in the icebox, then poured a glass of ice water and drank it so fast it made my head ache. That happens when I eat or drink something cold too fast.

"Why're you so red in the face?" she asked.

"It's hot out there," I said. "And the sheriff pretended to shoot me. I think he hates me."

"He hates everybody," said Lily. "He treats kids bad 'cause he can. In particular, colored kids. He might try to scare you, Brother, but that's all."

"Well, he sure tries," I said.

"You don't need to worry. Even the sheriff knows better than to do anything to you. He'd never get by with it. Not being who you are and all."

"What do you mean, who I am? I'm me."

"Brother Sayre, there's a big difference between you and some other folks. Your family name protects you. You're the judge's grandson and your mama's own chile. And you're white. You have noticed that, haven't you?"

"I don't feel any different," I said. "But heck, Lily, I don't know how he treats colored kids. I don't have any colored friends. Most of mine are friends from school or church. It's not my fault we've got a white school and a black school, and I go to the white one. That's just how it is."

"You're right," said Lily softly. "That's jest how it is."

I squashed a tiny green worm crawling out from the pile of corn husks.

"Don't be mashing that thing on my clean oilcloth," said Lily.

Chapter Three

A wisteria vine twined around the columns and roofline of the front porch. The silky purple flowers, like clusters of grapes, covered peeling paint, broken roof shingles, and rain-damaged eaves. Shirley Boligee lay stretched out in the vine's leafy shade. Swan and I were waiting for the train.

"I wish we were rich," said Swan. "Then I could have lots of dresses and a Shirley Temple doll with real hair."

"That's just plain silly," I told her, scratching the cat's belly with my toe.

Off in the distance, the train whistle wailed over the empty fields. The men would be here soon!

It wasn't long 'til our boarders came up the front path. Mr. E. L. Edwards, the engineer, and Dusty Rhodes, his fireman, wore hickory-striped overalls and railroad caps. Captain Wooten was dressed in a dark blue suit. He carried a tin lunch pail with "Conductor" stenciled on the top, a sheaf of newspapers under his arm, and a little bag that I knew held presents for Swan; he was always bringing her stuff from the dining car—menus, pink and green mints shaped like tiny hearts, and fancy napkins.

I've learned a lot about railroading since the men from the Southern Railroad started boarding with us. For instance, now I know that railroad men liked to be called by their initials. Only Dusty was called by his name. He said a man whose last name was Rhodes was bound to be given the nickname of Dusty, Muddy, or Crooked.

"I picked the best one," he said.

Dusty was skinny, with curly red hair that he tried to tame with Brylcreem hair tonic. His job as fireman is hard. He sits on the left side of the engine's cab, pivoting in a crouch while he shovels coal—black diamonds—between the tender and the fire. And he has to scatter the coals so the fire burns evenly.

"They don't come any better than Dusty," said Mr. Edwards. "He can place his shots in the firebox good as Babe Ruth hits baseballs."

Before I met Dusty, I didn't know what a firebox was. I'd been watching steam locomotives for as long as I can remember, but I never thought about how the steam got there. So I asked.

"It's the firebox that holds the fire that heats the water that makes the steam that runs the engine," Dusty explained. "The engineer pushes the throttle and controls the flow of steam down the main steam pipe to the engine.

And that's what moves the steam locomotive along the tracks and across the country."

Dusty knows a lot about mechanical things. He's also the only person who can keep our car, an old 1925 Maxwell, in running condition. I like him a lot, Captain Wooten too. But it's Mr. Edwards who's my hero. When he walks into a room, it seems to fill up with something good and strong.

Swan led the way into the hall. At the foot of the stairs, Mr. Edwards took out his pocket watch: a round, gold Bulova that he calls Jubilo. Opening it, he looked at the face and said, "We were right on time."

Folks around here set their watches by the train. Mr. Edwards said that that's why he'd named his watch Jubilo. It sends a message; it announces time. An engineer's watch is very important: It signals to him to make up time, or hold time back. It tells him if the train's running fast or slow.

"The way I look at it, a railroad engineer carries time in his pocket," said Mr. Edwards, handing me the watch. "Now, how 'bout taking Jubilo up to my room. I'll go tell your mama we're here."

Holding the watch and chain carefully, I went upstairs. In the light from the window, Jubilo shone like a small sun in the palm of my hand. When I grow up, I'm going to be a railroad engineer. I want to carry time in my pocket, too.

* * *

Mealtimes with the boarders are like big family dinners. At least I think they are. Our family's pretty small, but I can

18

imagine big families having dinners like ours. Mama puts a starched white tablecloth and fresh flowers on the dining room table. She and Lily cook different kinds of stuff too, so everybody's happy. Our meals are better because of having company.

After the blessing, Dusty tucked his napkin in his shirtfront, spooned up candied yams, and passed the bowl down the table.

"Did I tell y'all about my visit to the picture show?"

"Not more'n twice," said Captain Wooten. He's not really a captain, but he's called that because of the respect the train passengers have for him.

"Tell it anyway," said Swan, tracing her finger down the pitcher of iced tea that was beaded in the heat.

"I had a turnaround in Savannah, and some time to kill," said Dusty. "So I went downtown to the Lucas Theatre. It's a ritzy place—marble stairs, crystal lights hanging down, and velvet ropes across the doors."

"How'd you get in?" Swan asked, eating black-eyed peas one at a time.

"The usher took down the rope, sweetheart. While we were waitin' for the picture to start, a fella playin' a fancy organ come right up out the floor. Then the lights died down, and a Pathé newsreel started up."

He took a swallow of tea and continued his story.

"Ol' Adolph Hitler was up on a stage in front of thousands of folks, stickin' their arms up in the air to salute. The soldiers marched by all stiff-legged—goose-steppin' is what they call it. Now, what kind of way is that to march? If you ask me, Germans don't show good sense. Why,

Hitler's such a liar, he'd have to hire somebody to call his dog for him."

"I saw Hitler in a newsreel, too," I said. "He's goofy looking."

"He's a dangerous man," said Mr. Edwards. "All Nazis are dangerous."

The way he said it, I got a cold chill down my back. For a minute or so, nobody said anything, then Lily brought in biscuits, fresh out of the oven.

"We'll have to take up the problem of the Nazis later," said Captain Wooten. "Dusty'll be too busy chewin' to talk." His appetite for Lily's biscuits was famous.

After supper, the men went out to the front porch. When I finished my chores, I went out to join them. Katydids whirred in the fields with a metallic sound that nearly drowned out the slow creaking of rocking chairs. A light breeze freshened as the sun sank lower in the sky.

Dusty was sitting on the steps, talking about something that happened down at the railroad yard. "I wasn't there when it happened," he said, making room for me on the step. "But I trust P. B. Dixon to tell me the truth."

"Who's P. B. Dixon?" I asked.

"He's a Pullman porter on the railroad," said Dusty, "and a good man. Colored porters work the sleeping cars, you know, and Dixon heard the story over at the colored boardinghouse where he stays when he's in town."

"Brother," said Mr. Edwards softly, "keep in mind we're talking railroad business, and you know you aren't to say anything about what we talk about. It could get someone in trouble. You understand?"

"Yessir," I said.

"As I was saying," Dusty continued, "the sheriff's got no authority down in the yard. He's oversteppin' hisself, beatin' up hobos. It's the business of the railroad bulls to deal with hobos and tramps. And you don't need to beat 'em up."

"Was the man who was beaten white or colored?" Captain Wooten asked.

"Colored," said Dusty. "I don't believe it would make any difference to Hamm, long as he could beat up somebody. But he can get by with beatin' a colored man easier."

A few minutes later, I heard Mama and Swan coming down the hall. The men grew quiet. Mr. Edwards filled his pipe and looked out across the garden. The tobacco smoke smelled like cherries as it drifted over the railings.

When Mama and Swan were seated, Mr. Edwards began talking about driving the train, and some of the things that happened.

"There's music in the rails," he said in his deep voice. "You're beguiled by sounds and smells. You can hear a chorus of frogs in the ditches at blind sidings, and there's the smell of steam mixed with fresh-plowed earth. Best of all is the wonder of a 4-4-0 locomotive racing down the high iron with a mail contract at stake. That's when you hear the music of the rails!"

Taking a puff of his pipe, he said, "When you come right down to it, railroading's a fine life."

"Mr. Edwards," I said. "Do you think I could be a railroad man when I grow up?"

"I expect so," he said.

21

"I don't know," said Dusty. "How's your pitching arm?"

I couldn't tell if he was kidding or not. "Not too good," I said.

"Then I guess you won't be a fireman," he said.

It felt so good out there on the porch. I felt safe when the men were here. And I know one thing: I'm making a promise to myself that one day, that fine life will be mine, too. I'm going to race down the high iron, and listen to the music of the rails.

The sun slipped lower in the western sky, and the air cooled. Chimney swifts soared and darted just above the treetops. The men's voices wove a net of words that held us captive as the long day faded. When the first star pricked the sky, Swan made a wish.

Then we sat out on the porch, rocking the sun down.

Chapter Four

Morning mists ghosted the tracks and a plume of coal-smelling black smoke rose from the train's engine. Mr. Dupree, the stationmaster, gave the signal and Engine No. 111, carrying six freight cars, a mail and baggage car, and one passenger car, chugged down the tracks. I watched the train leave, then started back home.

Down the road, sharecroppers' houses sat scattered across the fields like pulled teeth. Sammy Linton lives in one of them. He's in my class at school this year. That's about the only place I ever see him, and he doesn't always show up there. Sammy's little and skinny and his hair looks like cotton. He comes to school barefooted and sometimes he has to go to the school nurse because of his bruises. Miss Riley, the school principal, sent a note home with him asking to see his parents, but they didn't come. I don't even know if Sammy's got a mama. If he does, I never saw her.

But he surely does have talent for making puppets. He carves them out of wood and their faces look real. He brought some to school to show us. One day, he asked me if my mama had any scraps of material he could have to make clothes for his puppets. Mama fixed up a box for him with leftover material from stuff she'd sewn: pajamas, a dress for Swan, pillowcases, and aprons.

I took the box to school for him, but the next day, Sammy brought it back. His pa told him that the Lintons didn't take charity from folks who think they're better than anybody else. I could tell Sammy felt bad about it.

When I told Mama what Mr. Linton had said, she was really mad.

"I *am* better than he is," she said. "The sorriest creature in the swamp is better. That old man's a drunk and he's mean to his family. Brother, you remember to be kind to Sammy."

"Yes, ma'am," I said.

Nobody knew how long the Lintons would be in Snow Hill. Sharecroppers live in mean houses for a season, then leave for another mean house in another season. They'd probably move after the summer picking season was over.

* * *

Even though it was early, the sun was already hot. Today was grass-cutting day, and I had to cut it. It wasn't easy on account of we've got a lot of it, and the lawnmower isn't worth a toot. It's an old push mower that I believe Noah used before he built the ark. I dragged the confounded thing from the shed out back and got started. But the blades were so dull that I had to stop to sharpen them. While I was trying to use the flat file, my sweaty hands and arms got crusted with rusty filings. I cut my finger and nearly filed off part of my thumb. A fly buzzed around my head, and when I tried to swat it, I hit my sore thumb on the lawnmower handle.

"That's it!" I said. "I quit!"

I went over to the spigot and splashed cold water over my face and head, then sat on the back steps to cool off. The sweet smell of blackberries cooking drifted through the screened door. I could hear Mama and Lily in the kitchen. They were making blackberry jelly and talking up a storm about somebody named Rose.

"She's had a hard row to hoe," said Lily. "First, that triflin' man of hers ran off and left her with a small boy to take care of, and she didn't even have a job."

Then they started talking real soft, and I couldn't hear what they said, even though I tried. I've learned a lot by eavesdropping, although Mama said that if you eavesdrop, you might hear something about yourself you won't like.

I went inside and hung my hat on the doorknob. "We need a new lawnmower," I said.

"That ain't all we need," said Lily.

"What's the matter?" I asked, not knowing for sure that something was.

"Brother," said Mama, "you don't have to know every single thing that goes on."

"I just asked," I said, taking the pitcher of ice water out of the icebox.

"Rose is Lily's sister," said Mama.

"Anyway," said Lily, "one day Rose saw an ad in a Negro paper sayin' things were better for coloreds in Detroit. She believed it and up and left Snow Hill. She got a job alright, but now she's lost it, and she's sending Champion to stay with Papa and me 'til she gets back on her feet again."

"Who's Champion?" I asked.

"Rose's son," said Mama, ladling purple jelly into pint jars.

"So, I don't know him either, right?"

"No, I don't reckon you would," said Lily. "That was before I came to work here."

About the time my daddy died. "Two years ago," I said. Mama looked over at me, her eyes shiny.

"How old is he?" I asked.

"Almost twelve, same as you," said Lily, pouring hot paraffin over the top of the jelly to seal it in the jars.

"Champion can be a big help on the farm," said Mama. "I have to believe it'll work out fine. They do say the Lord tempers the wind to the shorn lamb."

"I pray that's so, Miss Serena," said Lily, wiping her eyes on her apron.

Later, Mama explained that it wasn't that Lily didn't want her nephew to come for a visit. She was just worried about being able to take care of him.

"These days," Mama said, "keeping clothes on your back and food on the table are everyday troubles for most folks."

The Everlasting Now

Lily and her father, Jesse Luther, live in a farming community called Rabbit Yard that's within good walking distance of our house. Jesse's a farmer and a preacher at the Free Hope Baptist Church. It was there that Lily and her sister Rose had sung with a gospel group called The Five Golden Stars. After Rose left town, the group renamed itself The Five Golden Stars Minus One.

Jesse raises crops, chickens, and a few pigs. Most days, he makes a regular stop by the local café for scraps to feed his pigs. But times are so hard that if hobos get there first, the pigs lose out and have to make do with a few table scraps, corn husks, and peelings.

* * *

A few days later, I was standing under the chinaberry tree in the backyard. Sunlight shining through the leaves turned my skin green. Blue jays were setting up a fuss in the magnolia tree nearby and I was going to run 'em off with my slingshot.

I pulled back the sling, let her fly, and *whack!* I hit a boy I'd never laid eyes on before.

Lily yelled, "Brother! What is wrong with you? You crazy or what? You just hit Champion in the head! Get over here!"

"It was a pure accident," I said. "I was aiming at a blue jay."

"Well, your aim is off!" she said. "This is my nephew, Champion Luckey. And Champion, this is the strange person who lives in this house. His name is James Longstreet

Sayre and he's called Brother. Now if you'll excuse us for a minute, Brother and I are gonna have a little talk."

Which meant she'd talk and I'd listen. If Lily told Mama what I did, she'd kill me…or let Lily do it.

Lily took me off to a corner of the yard where she reminded me about the last time I got in trouble with my slingshot. I swear, she has a memory like an elephant. Just when you figure she's forgotten, she'll remind you of your past sins.

Last summer, a friend of Mama's was visiting from Selma with her son Dwayne. "Du-wayne" was how they said it. He was ten years old and the biggest creep I ever saw. He was sneaky, like one of those little slick dogs that come up behind and nip your ankles. I got him good. 'Course I got in trouble, and Mama took away my sling-shot for a while, but it was worth it.

"You didn't like him either," I said.

"His mama did spoil him rotten," said Lily. "Besides, anybody named Du-wayne is bound to spend serious time in a state prison. But then Champion ain't Du-wayne."

"I'm sorry, Lily, I didn't mean to hit him."

"Go tell him. He's the one got hit in the head," she said. "Now, hand it over."

"Aw, Lily, I spent a lot of time getting this slingshot just right." I'd rubbed the wood with sandpaper 'til it was smooth as powder. I'd made the sling out of a piece of old inner tube from the filling station.

I handed over my perfect slingshot. "How long are you gonna keep it?" I asked.

"As long as it takes for you to get smart," she said.

The Everlasting Now

Champion was waiting on the porch. He was kind of dressed up; his white shirt was buttoned to the top, his trousers were starched to a fare-thee-well, and he wore black high-top tennis shoes. His skin was lighter than Lily's. "What'd you shoot me with?" he asked.

"Slingshot," I said. "Well, a chinaberry from a slingshot. I'm sorry. Guess I zigged when I should have zagged." I didn't want to tell him that I couldn't always see what I was aiming at.

"It didn't hurt much," he said, rubbing his head.

Swan came out with her cat draped over her arm. "Mama's gon' be mad with you, Brother, shootin' at strangers. Lily told me." She smiled at Champion.

"My cat's name is Shirley Boligee. I named her after Shirley Temple, my favorite movie star. Boligee's the name of the town where my grandmother was born. Only she's dead now. What's your whole name?"

"Champion Always Luckey," he replied.

"Huh. It's almost as long as Brother's. Won't you have a seat?"

He rocked from one foot to the other, then sat down. He looked all around at Mama's garden, at the tall pole hung with hollow gourds for purple martins to nest in, and at the posts of the porch that needed painting.

"This is your home?"

"It used to belong to our grandfather," I said, "but he died. Now we live here."

"It's mighty big for just one family," he said.

"We got boarders," said Swan. "They take up a lot of room."

29

"I'm gon' be stayin' over by my Aunt Lily's and my grandpa's. He's alive. I rode the Greydog all the way from Detroit by myself."

I'd never heard the Greyhound bus called the Greydog before. I was impressed; it sounded tough. "That's a ways to come all by yourself," I said.

"Well, I didn't mind too much," he said.

Chapter Five

Mama dropped me off at the softball field across the street from our church. She was taking Swan to a little girl's birthday party.

"You can walk home when practice is over," said Mama, "or you can wait and ride home with us."

I'd rather walk. If I waited, I'd have to smile and be polite to all those ladies at the party.

Practice was miserable and I was, too. I'm not that great a ballplayer, and the whole team knows it. I only went 'cause there aren't any other kids out where we live, so softball practice for the church team is about the only time I see anybody I know, except for real church and that didn't count.

Once in a while I'd see a friend at the picture show, when I had a dime to buy a ticket. That didn't happen often. And it didn't do any good to ask for money unless you earned it. There wasn't enough to go around, and that's the truth. No matter what you ask for, the answer is always "We're living in the Depression."

The house was empty when I got home. It was Wednesday and Lily's afternoon off. I was sitting on the back steps when Champion came around the side of the house.

When he first came to stay with Lily and Jesse, Lily wouldn't let him come to our house at all. She was afraid that since he's colored and I'm white, some folks wouldn't like it if we were friends. It sounds kind of silly to me. Besides, Lily's like part of the family, and Champion's her nephew. Only difference for me was that I'd never had a colored friend before.

But Mama said it wasn't anybody's business what we did. That was the first time I'd known Mama to be dead wrong about anything. As it turned out, it seemed to be most everybody's business.

Champion sat on the steps next to me.

"Know what?" I said.

"What?"

"Softball stinks. And I don't think they want me on the church team. Coach Spellman didn't say that, but he called me over and said, 'It's no use, Sayre. You've got to move your feet; don't just stand in the outfield. Try to catch the ball.' I didn't tell him that half the time I can't even see the confounded ball 'til it's practically in my face. I'm no good at sports."

"I can show you how to catch," said Champion. "I'm a pro. Come on, get your ball and glove."

I was soon to learn that he considered himself a pro at

most things. He pitched the ball to me time after time, and time after time I missed it. In the afternoon heat, we were soon drenched with sweat. Thousands of gnats swarmed around my eyes and ears. Champion kept pitching, and I kept missing.

After the last missed pitch, he called out, "Hold it." Walking slow, he came across the yard and stood directly in front of me.

"Can you see me?" he asked.

"Sure, I can see you."

"Okay," he said, going back a little farther. "Now can you?"

"I can see you," I said. "It's the dang ball I can't see!"

"Squinch up your eyes," he said, "I'm gonna throw it." He took a few steps back, wound up, pitched, and hit me square in the head.

"I think you need glasses," he said, helping me to my feet.

I'd already figured that out, but we didn't have money for glasses. Besides, it wasn't that bad; mostly I just couldn't see things flying through the air at me.

We went into the kitchen for cold lemonade, then took our glasses out to the shade of the front porch.

Sammy Linton's pa was walking down the road in front of the house. He looked our way, then quick turned his head like he didn't see us. I know he did though, 'cause he looked back a couple of times like he was checking us out or something. He's strange. When he got down the road, I kind of wondered where he was going. Town's the other way.

"He looks like an ol' scarecrow," I said. "His son Sammy was in my class at school and I like him. But ol' man Linton is weird and mean. He's even mean to his own son."

"You got any cookies to go with this lemonade?" Champion asked.

"I don't know," I said. "Let's go see."

* * *

Not long after that, Mama asked how come I wasn't going to softball practice anymore. "Mr. Spellman asked about you," she said.

I told her I got tired of it, and I wasn't any good anyhow. "It's Champion who's good at softball," I said. "But he can't play on the team because he didn't go to my church, and because he's colored."

Mama said to do what I wanted about the softball team. If I didn't want to play, then to heck with it.

* * *

I'm getting to do lots of new things since Champion came to visit. Before, I didn't know much about fishing and neither did he. Now, his grandpa, Jesse Luther, is teaching us how.

Jesse's favorite fishing spot is upstream in the piney woods. He likes to use fat green Catawba worms for bait. We pick them off the Catawba tree out back of our house. At least, Jesse and I pick 'em. Champion won't touch one;

I even have to bait his hook for him. He doesn't like any-thing that crawls, except maybe lizards. At least I'm not scared of worms. I'm kind of scared of Lily though. If you're not going to use the worms right away, you have to keep 'em cool, and she has a pure hissy fit if she finds some in the icebox. They do stink.

Another thing Jesse's taught us is how to catch a snake, not that I ever wanted to. I hate snakes. One day he told us he needed a king snake to put in his barn to kill mice and other snakes. He said we could go with him if we didn't get in the way. Fat chance of that! We tagged along 'cause we didn't think he'd find one.

Jesse started out across his back pasture with a croker sack over his arm. Down by the pasture fence, a tallow tree had been struck by lightning and had fallen. Its branches stuck up the air like skeleton fingers. Easing over to the tree, Jesse motioned us to be quiet.

A big gray snake with reddish orange blotches down its back was wrapped tight around a dead branch. Moving slow, Jesse reached over and broke off the branch at the bottom. He brought the snake back to where we were standing.

"Holy moley!" said Champion.

"Will it bite?" I asked.

"No," said Jesse, "it's a rat snake. But one of you has to hold the sack while I drop him in."

Meanwhile, that ol' snake was looking around and didn't seem to like what he saw. Champion was already backing off. I could see he wasn't gonna be any help, so I said I'd do it.

Holding the rough sack open, I closed my eyes. I felt the snake drop to the bottom. Jesse quick tied a knot at the top of the sack so it couldn't escape.

When I opened my eyes, Champion was running across the pasture. He flew like the wind. He could run like a pro, too.

"Look at him go!" said Jesse. "Look at that boy go! He might grow up to be the new Jesse Owens."

"Dusty told me that at the Olympic games in Germany, ol' Hitler got so mad when Jesse won that he stomped out of the stadium," I said. "Guess he didn't want an American to win."

"He didn't want an American Negro to win," said Jesse with a grin.

Chapter Six

One morning Mama said she'd give Champion and me a dime each if we'd cut the grass. "It just looks awful," she said. "I'd be embarrassed for anybody to see it."

That was something new. I almost never got paid to cut grass. We were happy to be getting paid for anything, and there wasn't much we wouldn't do for a dime.

We took turns pushing the lawnmower, but it was hard work on account of that sorry thing. You'd push, hit something in the grass, and get poked in the stomach. I like to mow it in straight lines, but Brother liked circles best. Mama came out to look at it when we were through.

"It's certainly different," she said, giving us our money. We had enough to go to the picture show to see the new Tarzan movie.

The Roxy Movie Theatre was one of the few places in town still open for business. Mama said because things were so bad, folks needed to forget their worries even for a little while. So they went to the picture show and pretended things were better. I know I sure loved it.

Lily told us what to do when we got there. As if I didn't know—I've been going to that picture show since I was little. But what she was saying was what to do *now*.

"It's different this time, Brother," she said. "If you all are goin' to the picture show, you each go up to the ticket window by yourself. Don't go up together. You understand? Act like you don't know each other. Get your ticket and go in by yourselves. You can meet up afterwards."

Things sure got complicated when Champion and I became friends, and it's just because one of us is white and the other is colored. It doesn't make a particle of sense. I know this sounds dumb, but there are things I'd never noticed before, like separate water fountains and schools, and coloreds having to sit in the balcony at the picture show. It made me feel like I'd been asleep. Champion and I already knew we couldn't sit together. He had to sit in the balcony with the coloreds, while I sat downstairs. I would have liked to sit upstairs so I could watch folks better, but it wasn't allowed.

We saw a Bugs Bunny cartoon where Bugs had a mustache and stomped around like old Hitler, giving a Nazi salute. Then the Pathé newsreel came on showing Jesse Owens getting his gold medals at the Olympics. I remembered what Jesse said. "They didn't want an American Negro to win." Nazis stink, in my opinion.

"The Heavyweight Championship of the World"

flashed across the screen. There were boxing clips of Joe Louis and James Braddock, the contenders for the throne. The audience clapped when Joe Louis came on because he was from Alabama. We saw Joe Louis at his training camp with his manager, Chappy Blackburn, and James Braddock at his training camp.

Then the movie came on, and we watched Tarzan and Jane and Boy living in a tree house in the jungle. Cheetah, the family chimpanzee, was there, too.

When the show was over, I went across the street to wait for Champion. It was late afternoon and it was still hot. I sure could have used an ice cream cone, but I didn't have any more money. When the sheriff rode by in his Ford, I turned around and looked in the window of the dime store, pretending I didn't see him.

Then, out of the corner of my eye, I saw Mr. Linton walking down the alley next to the picture show. No matter what he's doing, he looks like he's hiding something; he gives me the creeps. I saw the sheriff's car reflected in the window as he stopped to pick up Mr. Linton. I was hoping he was getting arrested, but it didn't look like it.

When Champion came out of the picture show, I motioned to him to stay where he was. I didn't want the sheriff to see us together. When the Ford moved on, we waited 'til it was way down the street, then we started to walk home. "That's the man you've got to be careful of," I said.

"I know," he said. "Aunt Lily told me about him. This is a crazy town," he said. "I don't know many whites in Detroit, but it ain't as bad as this."

We talked about the championship fight that was coming up soon.

"You like Joe Louis?" Champion asked.

"Sure," I said. "Everybody likes Joe Louis."

"He came to my school in Detroit," he said.

"Did not!"

"Did too. Duffield Elementary. The teachers let us out of class to see him. Joe walked down the hall giving out presents."

I couldn't believe he'd seen Joe Louis in person. "Are you tellin' me the truth?"

"Cross my heart," he said. "I'm an expert on Joe Louis. For instance, his real name is Joe Louis Barrow. But when he filled out the papers for his first amateur fight, he wrote so big he couldn't fit his whole name on the card. Joe Louis is his *professional* name."

"I know that," I said. I didn't, but I said I did. "Did you know he was born over in the next county?"

"Yeah," he said, "Aunt Lily told me. He used to be real poor."

"Now he's a hero," I said.

"Well, just don't try to take him for your hero," said Champion.

"He's one of my heroes, along with Mr. Edwards. I been liking Joe for a long time."

"That's the problem," he said. "The whites want to take him for their hero. He belongs to us."

"To us who?"

"To the coloreds," said Champion. "He's the best hero we got, besides Jesse Owens."

"Well, you can share him, can't you?"

"I guess," he said. "I've got a secret about him."

"What is it?"

"I can't tell you," he said. "It's a secret."

"Will you tell me sometime?"

"Yeah, maybe," he said.

* * *

It was only a week until the big fight. Most folks didn't get to see them; they listened to them on the radio. But even listening wasn't always easy. Like everything else during the Depression, radios were scarce. Folks didn't have money to buy radios, or much else for that matter.

We were lucky to have the small radio in the kitchen, and the Grundig console that had been my grandfather's. Some folks had to leave home to find a radio to listen to. There was one at Mr. Harper's store, and he stayed open late on fight nights so folks could sit in the store and listen.

"Whites can sit in the store and listen," said Lily. "Coloreds have to sit or stand outside near a window."

That sure surprised me. I've been going to Harper's Goods & Feed since I was little. The outside walls have signs advertising Red Man Chewing Tobacco, Dr Pepper, Tube Rose Snuff, and Prince Albert Tobacco.

Inside the store, they sell lard, canned food, yard goods, animal feed, sugarcane, and most anything else you need. I'd always liked Mr. Harper, but he wasn't being fair about that radio.

One afternoon, while Mama and Lily were busy

upstairs, I sneaked into the hall to use the telephone. I held a handkerchief over the receiver to disguise my voice, and called Mr. Harper's store.

"Do you have Prince Albert in a can?"

"Yes, we do," said Mr. Harper.

"Well, you best let him out. He can't hear the radio in there. Like some other folks."

I hung up, then heard a noise behind me. Lily was standing on the stairs. She walked on down the hall and right past me like she didn't see me. I believe she saved me a lot of trouble with Mama.

* * *

June 22, 1937, was the night of the big fight. Our boarders would be staying with us that night, so Mama decided to have a Championship party. The only other railroad man in town was Mr. Dupree, the stationmaster. Even at the smallest station, the depot agent was expected to look after everything to do with trains and keeping customers happy. Mama asked me to take the invitation down to him, to see if he could join us.

The railroad depot was my favorite building in town. Painted dark red with white trim, it had a neat garden on the side away from the rails. The platform smelled of creosote and of sawdust burning slow from the sawmill.

The stationmaster's office seemed to hold all the secrets of the universe. It was nearly as fine as the cab of an engine. On top of the rolltop desk were ticket rolls, a ticket validator, and copies of *The Official Guide* and *The Book of Rules*. A Seth Thomas clock with a big, round face hung on one wall. Next to it was the hoop used for passing orders to the engineer as the train passed. The telegraph sat on the ledge of the bay window, its brass keys shining in the sunlight.

Mr. Dupree was a telegrapher, what railroad men called a "brass pounder." Since he knew Morse code, he was the first person in town to get news from the outside world—when there was any news from the outside world.

He was what Mama called "dapper." He wore starched white shirts and dark suits and lived upstairs over the depot in rooms furnished by the railroad. Mama had told Lily that Miz Edna Earl had Mr. Dupree in her sights.

"She's bent on marrying him," said Mama, "and wants him to move out of his rooms and into her house."

Heck fire, I'd rather live in a boxcar like Lucius than live anywhere with Miz Edna Earl. I sure wouldn't leave rooms over the depot for her, maybe not for anybody.

Chapter Seven

The Free Hope Baptist Church sat out in a grassy field dotted with wildflowers. In late afternoon, the sinking sun changed the plain square steeple to gold. A few mule wagons were parked under shade trees. There weren't any cars parked there, 'cause nobody had one. Folks walked or rode in a mule wagon. Jesse's mule Nicodemus swatted flies with his braided tail.

Champion had invited me to Jesse's church for evening services. I'd been there before with Lily, who said our family was always welcome. "But most whites aren't," she said. "And it's because we feel like we have to 'put on a face' for them. It goes back to slavery days when church was the only place we could go to get away for a little while. In our church, or worship house, our people didn't have to share with anybody but God."

Even if it was in the olden days, I couldn't imagine Lily ever being a slave, as bossy as she is.

The Everlasting Now

Champion met me at the church steps, and we went inside. The lemony sweetness of honeysuckle drifted through the open windows. Carved above the altar were the words "One Lord, One Faith, and One Baptism." A large lady in a flowered dress was playing the piano. Lily sat in the choir section with The Five Golden Stars Minus One.

Jesse Luther stepped up to the altar. He looked different in his preaching clothes. His starched white shirt gleamed like snow in the overhead light. When he welcomed everybody, his voice sounded deep, like it came from somewhere in his innards. I remembered what Lily had said: "Preachers need a voice loud enough for God to hear on high, and deep enough to scare Satan down below."

He preached about how the Archangel Michael had defeated Lucifer, the Devil, in heaven, and had thrown him over the banister of time. When he finished and said a prayer, a chorus of soft "amens" slipped through the congregation like strung beads.

When it was time to take up the collection, Champion stepped out of the pew and walked up the center aisle, looking straight ahead. He began passing the collection basket down each pew to a deacon at the other end. It was called a "love offering" and taken up to help the sick and the needy.

Then the choir stood up to sing and the congregation joined in. Since the church was a poor one, there weren't enough hymnals to go around. So the choir director "lined" the hymn. He'd call out a line, and the congregation would repeat it in song. Everybody sang and clapped their hands in time to the music. Champion sang with a true voice. I guess he's a pro at singing, too. When the next hymn began, the lady sitting next to me took my hand and led me out into the aisle.

"When we praise the Lord," she said, "we praise the Lord!" I'm not a real good singer, but I am loud, and I can carry a tune. It's funny, but 'til then I'd never thought about enjoying church. At First Presbyterian where we go, everybody just stands up in their pews and sings. They don't even sing very loud.

* * *

The next day, after I finished hoeing weeds in the vegetable garden, I was dying for a glass of tea. Mama and Lily didn't even look up when I came into the kitchen. I poured a glass of tea and drank it standing at the sink. Mama was greasing cake pans and flouring them.

"When you finish that, Brother," she said, "find something to do, and get out from underfoot. Lily and I have work. The party's tomorrow night, remember?"

As if I could forget. But it wasn't the party I was thinking about, it was the boxing match. It seemed as if everything that happened since school was out was just leading up to the big fight.

"Can I go out to the farm to see Champion?" I asked.

"If it's all right with Lily," said Mama.

"You can go if you'll help and not hinder," said Lily,

looking up from the bowl of golden batter she was stirring. She was making a lemon pound cake for the party. "Champion's got work to do. He's gathering eggs and slopping the hogs before Papa gets back from town. And don't y'all go off anywhere."

Boy, she gives orders better than a sergeant in the U.S. Army. "We won't," I said. "There's no place to go."

* * *

Out at the farm, Nicodemus was cropping clover at the edge of the split-rail fence. The mule was fifteen hands high and had a coat the color of a Hershey bar. His braided tail swished back and forth like a whip. Jesse said that Nicodemus was the smartest mule in the county.

"Some folks say that a mule's jest stubborn, but that means they don't know a thing about 'em," he said. "You can't lead a mule. He won't be pulled, hurried, worried, or cuffed about. Mules are smart, smarter than horses. If he won't do somethin' you want, he's got a good reason. You can't make a mule do somethin' he don't feel is right. My Nicodemus is smart as a whip. He's my best companion."

Nicodemus came over to the fence and nuzzled my palm with his soft lips. I think he knows I like him. Guess I should've brought him a treat, but I didn't think about it when I left the house.

Champion came from the side yard carrying two empty buckets. "I'm through slopping the hogs," he said. "I just have to wash these out. I'll be right back."

When he returned a few minutes later, he stayed back from the fence.

"What's the matter?" I asked him. "Don't you like Nicodemus?"

He shrugged. "Not 'specially," he said. "Don't like hogs, don't like mules."

"I guess since you're from the city, you don't know 'bout mules." I didn't either, but I acted like I did.

"I know plenty 'bout this one," he said. "I *learned* plenty about him. I know cain't nobody but Grandpapa ride him. Try, and he'll roll over on his back. He loves to roll. Grandpapa said all mules love to roll. And he's liable to sit down anywhere, anytime. You can be comin' in from the pasture and he'll just sit. He poots a lot, too."

"Champion, do you think animals have souls? Our preacher's always talking about souls. He says everybody has one. You reckon Nicodemus does?"

"If he does, it's a wicked one," he said.

"Animals can't be wicked," I said. "What's your grandpa say about it? He's a preacher."

"I ain't ever asked about that mule's soul," said Champion as we walked up to the house.

The unpainted house and tin roof were the color of old silver. Red geraniums and pink cockscomb plants in lard buckets lined the wide front porch.

It was so hot that we went straight to the backyard and the water pump. Champion began yanking the handle up and down, up and down, until a stream of cool water gushed from the spout. With our mouths open, we drank the clear, cold water that tasted of iron. Then we splashed it over our heads and necks.

Afterwards, I looked around the place. A string of red and green peppers hung on a nail at the back door. When I asked about them, Champion said, "My grandpa eats 'em with his greens."

"Do you?" I asked.

"Sure," he said. "I love hot peppers. Cain't be too hot for me!"

I didn't believe him. "I double-dog dare you to eat one right now."

"Double-dog dare?" Champion turned away, took a swallow of water, shook the metal cup, and hung it back on its nail. Then he sauntered over to the porch and picked a small red pepper from the string. Holding it up, he closed his eyes, then popped it into his mouth.

His eyes flew open. He jumped straight up in the air, put his hands to his mouth, and ran to the water pump.

"Help me!" he croaked.

I started pumping for all I was worth. I pumped 'til the cold water gushed over his head, and he drank and drank, the water running down his chin. When he could speak, he gasped, "I don't know how Grandpapa does it!"

We sat for a minute while he recovered. Then he said, "I guess I'll show you my secret now."

We went into the kitchen that was clean and kind of bare. A Mason jar filled with yellow and orange flowers sat on the white tin-topped table. The walls were papered with newspapers. I'd been to Lily's house before, but I guess I'd never paid much attention to the walls.

"How come there's newspapers on the wall?"

"I don't know," said Champion. "It was like that when I got here. Now, close your eyes."

I did, and he went into another part of the house. "You got 'em closed?" he called.

"Yeah," I said, squeezing my eyes tight.

"Okay," he said a moment later, "now open 'em!"

He stood in front of me holding Joe Louis in a bottle. Only it wasn't really a bottle, it was the kind of jug that apple cider comes in—a demijohn. Blue modeling clay was smoothed over the bottom of the glass, and in the center, a small figure of Joe Louis was surrounded by little paper American flags.

I'd never seen anything like it. "Where'd you get the little statue?" I asked.

"Detroit," he replied, moving his hands over the curving sides of the bottle. "They sell 'em at the stores. Joe's the biggest hero in that town."

"Did you make this all by yourself?" I asked.

"Every single bit," he said.

"It's a mighty fine thing."

* * *

The next day, Mr. Edwards brought the train in about sunset. At supper that night, Dusty spooned up the last bite of apple cobbler. When Lily came into the dining room to remove the dessert bowls, he looked at me across the table and winked.

The Everlasting Now

"Anybody here care to place a little wager on tomorrow's fight?" he asked.

"What's the bet?" she asked.

"That James Braddock will knock out Joe Louis in the sixth round," he said.

Lily put the bowls back down on the table and looked at him, like she couldn't believe what she was hearing. "I'll take that bet," she said. "My terms are that I'll fix you all the biscuits you can eat, and make your favorite pie, but you got to put up cash money."

I couldn't believe my ears. Jesse'd have a fit if he knew Lily was gambling. But it probably didn't count 'cause she wasn't betting any money, just food.

After the others left the dining room, I said, "You're not betting against Joe, are you?"

"Guess I have to this time," said Dusty. "Jim Braddock's the 'Cinderella Man,' comin' back time after time, winning when some folks had given up on him. I like Louis too, he's a good fighter, but what I like most is gettin' a rise out of Lily by bettin' against Joe."

You don't know her like I do, I thought. *It's best to stay on her good side.*

* * *

Later that evening, we all sat out on the veranda. Mr. Edwards had brought out the floor lamp from the parlor and opened a book with a blue cover.

"These are essays," he explained. "Kind of like short stories, only they're real. They were written by a famous writer named Morley, and they're about all sorts of things. These are about railroads.

"It says here that in 1830, an English actress named Fanny Kemble saw her first steam engine. Here's what she said. 'This brave little she-dragon...the magical machine with its wonderful white breath.'

"Of course in those days," he said, "steam engines were smaller."

"Wish I could see a she-dragon," said Swan.

"Tell Brother about the *Flying Scotsman*," said Dusty. "She could fly a hundred miles an hour."

"How about the *Twentieth Century Limited*?" I asked.

But that's when Mama said it was time for bed for Swan and me.

"Tell everybody good night," she said.

It's tough being a kid.

Chapter Eight

The parlor doors were opened onto the veranda on the warm, bloomy night. Mama had spread a bridge cloth over a card table. On it were a vase of flowers, a pitcher of iced tea, and Lily's lemon pound cake in all its golden glory.

Mr. Dupree arrived with a box of Whitman's Sampler chocolates. I kept my eye on it. If Swan got to it first, she'd pinch each piece to see what was inside, then leave the kind she didn't like.

Mr. Edwards was in charge of the radio. Snow Hill was far from any major radio station, so a lot of expert dialing had to be done. Static across those airways sounded like winds out of the North Pole. Voices drifted in and out, and there had to be a sure hand at the controls to bring them back. Whoever was in charge spent a lot of time on one knee, tuning the dials for the best reception.

According to the boxing experts, which included nearly everyone, the fighters were pretty well matched. James Braddock became contender for the heavyweight crown when he beat Art Lasky. Then in an upset, he beat the champion, Max Baer, and took the title. Joe Louis was the first contender to challenge for the heavyweight title in two years.

Mama, who didn't like prizefighting, sat out on the veranda with Lily, who did. Champion and I stationed ourselves in the doorway. Swan was out in the garden catching fireflies in a Mason jar.

"If a lightnin' bug gets in the house, it means it's gonna storm," she caroled, her voice light as a calling bird's.

"Be quiet, Swan," I said. "It's gettin' ready to start!"

Mr. Edwards took Jubilo from his pocket and checked the time. The radio was turned on to warm up.

From Chicago's Comiskey Park, the sound of 42,000 boxing fans crashed across the airways like giant waves against the shore. The announcer told something about each fighter, then some experts on boxing talked about which man was favored to win.

"I wish they'd shut up and get on with it," I whispered to Champion.

Finally, the fight began. Braddock came out fighting and threw the first punch, a hard right that missed Joe's chin and hit his chest. Then Joe began jabbing—*right! left! right! left!* At the end of the first round, Braddock threw a short right uppercut at Joe's chin, knocking him to the canvas.

Champion jumped to his feet. "Get up, Joe!" he shouted. "Get up!"

The Everlasting Now

We were stunned. Was it possible that the great Joe Louis could lose?

"Louis is up again!" the announcer said. In the second round, Joe was winning. By the third, Braddock complained that the lights hurt his eyes. At the end of the sixth, his manager said he was ready to throw in the towel to stop the fight. But Braddock wouldn't let him.

"If you do, I'll never speak to you again!" he said.

By the eighth round, Joe had Braddock on the ropes. The boxers traded jabs, but the champion's were weak. Then Joe threw a powerful overhand right to Braddock's jaw and he fell facedown onto the canvas. There was a second of silence. The announcer yelled, "The winner and new heavyweight champion! Joe Louis!"

We couldn't see the fans, but we could hear their cheers as the entire Chicago audience rose to its feet. Lily squealed and jumped up from the glider. Mr. Dupree and Mr. Edwards pounded each other on the back. Champion started a victory dance around the veranda. I joined him, then Swan came in from the yard and started dancing, too. She yelled "*Ya! Ya! Ya! Ya! Ya!*" 'til I told her to shut up. Mama gave me a look and went in to cut the cake.

As soon as word of Louis's victory was out, everybody started celebrating. His fans clogged streets, shouting, ringing cowbells, and beating pots and pans. They said later on the radio that in New York City, over five thousand people marched up Seventh Avenue in a victory parade for Joe. That's more people than we've got in our whole town. What a night!

Lily collected on her wager with Dusty and said she was going shopping for new silk roses for *her* old hat.

* * *

By the next day, it was all over but the shoutin'. Champion came over to the house with Lily. We'd been promised a dime each to weed the vegetable garden and pick a mess of butter beans, but he was still celebrating Joe Louis's victory. He was out in the garden shadowboxing the bean vines, throwing punches in the air...*bap! bap! bap!*

"Champion," I said, looking up from the row of beans. "I ain't earning your dime, too." I'd weeded by myself, but I wasn't going to pick beans by myself. I set a bushel basket down by the vines growing thick over chicken-wire fencing.

"You ever pick butter beans?" I asked.

"Nope," he said. "They come already picked and canned in Detroit. Aunt Lily said to watch and do what you do."

Shirley Boligee was chasing yellow butterflies through the cabbage patch, and Swan was chasing Shirley. A few minutes later she picked up the cat and came over to us.

"It's too hot out here," she said. "We're goin' in where it's cool."

"She's so spoiled," I said, "and it's just 'cause she's a girl."

For a while, we worked in silence. My back was soaking wet. I batted at a swarm of gnats tormenting me around my eyes. I looked over at Champion. A drop of sweat trembled at the tip of his nose.

"You're supposed to watch and do what I do?" I said.

56

The Everlasting Now

He nodded, brushing at gnats.

I looked in the basket to see how many beans we'd picked. "I'll tell you what you can watch me do. You can watch me quit! And you can quit with me!"

"Yeah," he said, dropping a handful of beans into the basket. "Don't nobody need that many beans!"

Lily met us at the back door. "Don't y'all be comin' in my clean kitchen with your nasty selves," she said. "Just hand me the basket and go wash up at the spigot. I'll bring tomato sandwiches out to the porch for your lunch."

* * *

Later, we sat out on the veranda waiting for *The Lone Ranger,* our next-to-best radio program, to start. Our very best was *The Shadow,* starring the great detective, Lamont Cranston, but that came on in the evening.

Green hummingbirds, shiny as glass, darted in and out of the honeysuckle vines on the railings. Swan came out with Shirley Boligee in her arms. She'd dressed her in a baby doll dress and bonnet.

Champion looked up from a Joe Palooka comic book. "Whooee!" he said, "that is one ugly baby! The only one I ever saw with whiskers!"

Just then, a man on the radio began to sing. "You must have been a beautiful baby…you must have been a beautiful child…"

I laughed so hard my stomach hurt. Champion was practically falling out of the chair. Tears rolled down his face.

57

Upset at being the object of so much attention, Shirley jumped from Swan's arms and crawled under a chair. She stared out at us, her face framed by the ruffled bonnet.

We were still laughing when Mama and Lily came out with a colander filled to the brim with butter beans. They sat down, spread newspapers on their laps, and started shelling. The notes of a xylophone poured from the radio, cool as rain.

Champion stood up and began to dance. He moved as if on strings held by an invisible puppet master; his feet barely touched the floor. He dipped and swayed like somebody in a trance.

When the music died, we all clapped. Champion took a bow, and Mama and Lily went back inside.

"That was the Duke," said Champion.

"What duke?" I asked.

He looked at me, opened his mouth to speak, then slapped himself on the side of his head like he was trying to clear it. "White boys don't know nothin' about music," he said.

"White boy?" I asked, confused. "Why're you calling me a white boy?"

"I didn't mean it," he said. "But Duke Ellington is a famous musician. And he's a friend of Joe Louis's. You never heard of the 'A' Train?"

Now, I was the expert on trains, but I didn't know about any A train. "Is the duke an engineer too?" I asked.

Champion let out a howl. Shirley scooted out from under the rocking chair and dashed across the floor like a small ghost.

The Everlasting Now

"Now look what you did!" yelled Swan.

Champion shut his eyes like he was in pain.

"Brother," he said, "you don't ride the 'A' Train. It's music. You listen to it."

Chapter Nine

On Saturday, we hitched a ride to town with Jesse and Lily; we had money to spend. Riding in the back of a mule wagon filled with squash, yellow corn, and Rocky Ford melons isn't the easiest thing in the world, but it beats walking.

"Don't be messin' around back there," said Jesse. "My produce is for the market, not for you boys to sit on."

I noticed that he didn't have to give directions to Nicodemus.

"How does he know the way?" I asked.

"He could find the market with his eyes closed," replied Jesse.

"That's one smart mule," I said.

"Yes, he is," said Jesse, pleased that someone else saw his mule's good qualities.

Farmers from all over the county brought their produce to the town square on Saturdays. The backs of trucks and wagons were piled with corn, onions, okra, beans, tomatoes, and every kind of fruit that grew in the area, especially peaches and melons.

Jesse parked the wagon in the shade near the court-house. While we helped him put out his produce, Lily said she had some shopping to do. "When you all finish here, meet me at the tree that owns itself. In one half hour, you hear? And don't let the time slip up on you."

The market was really busy and local farmers, both col-ored and white, went about their business. A group of old men played checkers in the shade in front of the court-house. Shoppers milled around, talking to people they knew and looking at the wares offered for sale. One lady was selling baskets of brown turkey figs. Next to her, a lady had a table set up where she sold patchwork pillows and upside-down rag dolls.

When we finished helping Jesse set out his produce, he reminded us that we were supposed to meet Lily at the oak tree that owned itself. "Don't keep her waiting," he said. "You know how she is."

We wandered around looking at stuff but we weren't too interested in vegetables. Across the way, I saw Sammy Linton walking along, eating a peach. It was the first time I'd seen him since school was out. He was by himself. I looked to see if his hateful daddy was around, but I didn't see him.

"Come on, Champion," I said. "Let's go see Sammy. He's the one I told you about."

Sammy seemed glad to see me, but he looked bad. His overalls were patched and dirty and he smelled hot, like copper pennies. He nodded to Champion, then we stood there talking for a minute.

"I made some new puppets, Brother," he said. "One of 'em looks like President Roosevelt. Like that picture of him in our classroom. I'd show 'em to you, but I stay kinda busy." He kept looking around, like he was nervous or something. Then I saw why.

Mr. Linton was leaning against a truck, looking out over the crowd, when he spotted us. Suddenly, he stood up straight, looked hard, then started toward us.

When Sammy saw him making his way over to us, he said, "Y'all better git!"

"Come on, Brother!" said Champion. "Hurry!" Then he slipped away into the crowd, but I wasn't fast enough. Suddenly Mr. Linton was right in front of Sammy and me. Grabbing Sammy hard by his arm, he shoved him away from me. "Git outta here, boy!" he said. Sammy ran like the devil was after him.

Then getting up real close to me, old man Linton leaned down and pushed his ugly, unshaven face close to mine. "Nigger lover!" he whispered, his spittle spattering my face. Then he was gone.

For a minute I just stood there, frozen. It seemed like time stopped. I didn't know what to do. I looked around to see if anybody had noticed, but I don't think they did.

I went back to Jesse's wagon. Champion was already there, helping Miss Eulalie pick out a melon. When she saw me, she looked at me kind of hard. I must have looked funny 'cause she asked me if I was all right.

"Yes'm," I said, "just hot."

I put a Rocky Ford melon and some yellow crookneck squash into the string bag she held out. As she was leaving, she said, "Give your mama my best, Brother. Tell her I asked about her and that I'm savin' that book she wanted. It's *Rebecca*, by Daphne du Maurier."

"Yes'm," I said. I figured I could remember *Rebecca*, but I knew I'd never remember the author's name. I was trying to be polite, but I felt like I was gonna be sick. As soon as she was gone, I went over and washed my face in the public fountain. I didn't care who liked it or not. When I got back, Jesse reminded us about meeting Lily.

As we walked down the sidewalk, Champion said, "That man didn't hurt you, did he?"

"No," I said. "He's mean but he's not stupid enough to try that where folks could see him."

"He's scary," said Champion.

The day was ruined for me. I didn't want to stay, but we'd promised to meet Lily. I had to stay or tell her what happened. And I didn't want to do that.

* * *

The deep shade under the post oak tree was cool as an old room. There was a brass plaque sticking in the ground.

I, Winslow Herman Puckett, as Mayor of the City of Snow Hill, do hereby grant, bargain, sell and convey unto the "Post Oak Tree" as a creation, and a gift from the Almighty, to have and to hold itself, its branches, limbs, trunk and roots so long as it shall live.

"I never heard of a tree owning itself," said Champion.

When Lily got there, she looked at me kind of sharp. "Why's your hair wet, Brother?"

"I got hot," I said. I wasn't about to tell what happened.

"I'm going over to Miss Aletha's shop to buy silk roses for my hat," she said. "Do you all still have your dimes? Make up your minds how you're goin' to spend 'em, then meet me back here in half an hour. Don't get into trouble, you hear me?"

I didn't figure I could get into any more trouble than I already had.

On our way to Crumley's Drugstore, we passed Mr. Godbolt's insurance office, which was open, and the Mercantile Bank, which was closed. My daddy's newspaper office was closed too, but Eaton's Funeral Parlor was still in business.

The drugstore was dusky and cool, and smelled like vanilla and antiseptic. There was no one there except Doc Phinizy. He was standing at the marble soda fountain, filling the syrup dispensers. He's not a real doctor, but he is a real pharmacist, so everybody calls him Doc. His white jacket was reflected in the mirror behind him. Hanging above it was a hand-lettered sign.

WE RESERVE THE RIGHT
TO REFUSE SERVICE TO ANYONE.

"Who's this?" Doc asked me, nodding in Champion's direction.

"Lily Luther's nephew, Champion," I said.

Doc nodded, then went back to pouring syrup into a container.

We finally made up our minds about what we wanted. I ordered two double-dip strawberry cones. While Champion waited for them, I went over to the magazine rack to look at the latest Dick Tracy comic book.

"Don't read 'em if you're not buyin'," said Doc. "You'll get 'em sticky."

He always said that. A minute or so later, the screened door opened and shut.

"Hey, you, boy! What you think you doin', settin' at that counter?"

I looked over and saw Sheriff Hamm standing over Champion, pointing to the sign over the mirror.

"I asked you a question, boy!"

Champion was sitting on the stool like he was frozen. Our ice cream cones dripped in pink rivulets through his fingers.

The sheriff reached for his blackjack.

"There's no need of that!" said Doc. "I'm not having that kind of behavior in my store."

Fear rose up in my throat and tasted of bile. I dropped the comic book, ran over to Champion, and grabbed him by his arm. "C'mon!"

When we reached the sidewalk, Champion was still holding the ice cream cones. I grabbed one, but a second later, the ice cream fell off into the gutter. Racing down the street, we ran smack into Lily.

"What's the matter?" she said. "What happened?"

I told her. "And we weren't doing anything wrong! Honest, Lily! Champion was just sitting there, and I was looking at funny books."

She looked toward the drugstore. Sheriff Hamm was standing at the door. When he saw her, he turned his head and spat on the sidewalk.

"Let's go," she said.

We walked back over to the courthouse. "Are we going to get a ride with Jesse?"

I was hoping she'd say yes, but she didn't say anything, just kept on walking. I felt like I was drowning. I'd heard about people going down for the third time, and that's how I felt. My hands were sticky with ice cream, I was hot, and I was mad. I couldn't believe that everything that happened, *had* happened. I was minding my own business, not bothering anybody. Then old man Linton showed up and embarrassed me in public. Then the stupid sheriff showed up and was going to hurt Champion, and what did I do? I ran. That's what.

"I declare, Brother," said Lily. "Sometimes you don't think straight. How come you let Champion sit down at that counter? You should have waited for the ice cream cones yourself."

"What?" I said.

"Didn't you see that sign?"

The sign, the sign? Then I remembered. *We Reserve the Right to Refuse Service to Anyone.* "But Lily, I thought it meant drunks, and…well, folks acting out."

The Everlasting Now

Lily stopped dead in her tracks and put her shopping bags down. She'd been walking so fast her breath came in little puffs. "I doubt the sheriff would have told *you* not to sit at the counter."

"He might," I said. "I told you he hates me."

"This ain't about you," she said. "*Coloreds* are not allowed to sit at that counter, or any counter in any store in this town. Our money's good, long as we *stand* at the counter."

I took a deep breath. "Well, Doc ought to take that stupid sign down," I said. "It's not right."

Champion hadn't said a word since we left the drugstore. Now he said, "I don't like nobody callin' me 'boy' like that."

For the life of me, I couldn't understand why that worried him. I'd been scared stiff the sheriff was gonna do something horrible, like beat the livin' tar out of him with his blackjack.

"But Lily, I didn't know what the sign meant, and that's the truth! Champion didn't know either! Does Mama know about the sitting thing?"

"Brother," said Lily. "Miss Serena's the finest lady I know. She's kind and thoughtful. But I don't expect she ever really saw those signs. They don't *overwhelm* her like they would if she wasn't white. You understand? Most folks in this town, even the good ones, are *used* to how things are. They don't see anything wrong with 'em."

Handing each of us a shopping bag, she said, "Come on, let's see if Papa's ready to go."

"When we get home, I'm telling Mama about the signs. She's gonna be mad."

"Don't be tellin' your mama a thing," said Lily. "She's got enough on her mind, and there's nothin' she can do about how things are. Just let it be. Charge it to the dust and let the rain settle on it."

Chapter Ten

But I didn't let the rain settle on it. All afternoon I thought about how Champion looked with the sheriff standing over him. I decided to tell Mama about what happened at the drugstore, even if Lily killed me.

It was getting on toward that time between day and night that I only liked when the railroad men were here. Without them, the house felt too big and lonely. The air was still, windows open to catch any breeze that might happen along. A whippoorwill called from the magnolia tree, sounding lost and mournful.

Mama was in the sewing room. She was making a new dress for Swan out of one of her old party dresses. In the dusk, the light from the sewing machine shone like a tiny star. I didn't see Swan, which was good 'cause I didn't want her to hear what I had to say.

I didn't know where to start, so I started with Mr. Linton. As I talked, Mama measured the hem of Swan's new dress, slipping straight pins in a shining row in the crisp pink material.

"He called me that word we're not allowed to say."

She looked up from her sewing. "Which word?"

I whispered in her ear.

"That man's an ignorant redneck," said Mama. "It's typical of his kind that he'd pick on someone who couldn't fight back. Since he's about as low-down as you can get, he needs a scapegoat. He's picked Champion and got you in the bargain. I'm surprised he even approached you in the daytime, with other people around. Men like that usually do their worst at night, wearing sheets."

That was a scary thought. "Is he a member of the Ku Klux Klan?" I asked.

"I don't know," said Mama, "but he's the kind of trash that is."

Then I told her what happened in the drugstore. "Champion was just waiting for our ice cream cones! It's all because of that stupid sign, and because the sheriff just likes to pick on kids, 'specially colored kids, I guess."

"Lily was afraid something bad would happen if you two boys were friends, but I didn't think so," said Mama. "I thought that what we did was our business. Maybe I was wrong. I know that our family is different from a lot of families here. My father—your grandfather—was a fair judge. He once received death threats and hate mail when he ruled in court in favor of a colored man who'd been cheated by a powerful white man. But good people respected him. Just as they did your daddy when he wrote about racial or religious intolerance, even if they didn't

70

always agree with him." She folded the half-finished dress and laid it aside.

"Most people won't pay any attention to you and Champion being friends. Especially since Lily works for us and Champion's her nephew. Everybody knows us and about us. But there are others, like Mr. Linton, who behaves the way he does because he's a hater. He and the sheriff are both spoilers. What they don't understand, they want to wreck.

"And you or anybody else should be able to have a friend who's different, whatever the difference might be. But at this time, black and white friendships are not always approved of in our... community."

"We don't live in a community, do we?" I asked. "I mean, we live in the country."

"Not far enough country," she said. Mama pulled her hair back and twisted it into a soft knot on her head.

"I don't respect the sheriff. He's been a troublemaker since he got here. I believe he's using you as an excuse to pick on Champion. And he can, or he feels like he can, because Champion's colored. Tell me this," she said, "how did the sheriff happen to be in the drugstore? Did he just walk by and see Champion sitting at the counter?"

"I don't know," I said. "I didn't see him come in. I was looking at funny books. Then I heard him talking about that sign and scaring Champion because he was sitting instead of standing at the counter."

"Good Lord," said Mama, smoothing the hair away from my forehead with cool fingers. She was looking at me with her greeny-gray eyes like she hadn't seen me in a long time. "There's something more to all this that I don't understand. Something bad is going on in this world, and it's not just the Depression. It's as though something's been turned loose, something threatening. I heard on the radio today that the Japanese have seized Shanghai and Nanking."

I couldn't see what Japan and China had to do with us. "All I know is that the day of the big fight was one of the best days of my life," I said. "And today was one of the worst!"

Swan appeared in the faint gloom of the doorway. She was wearing red lipstick and it was crooked. I guess she'd been playing lady.

"The sheriff's mean and I hate him!" she said.

"I thought you were in your room," said Mama. "Come on over here by me. I don't know what you heard, but I don't want you to hate anybody. You can hate how they act, but not the person."

"Yes, ma'am."

"Now, go wash that lipstick off, and we'll go downstairs. You two go on into the parlor. It's almost time for *Fibber McGee and Molly.* I'll be there in a minute. I have to make a phone call first."

From the parlor, we could hear the thin peeping of tree frogs through the open doors of the veranda. Mama went down the hall to use the telephone. I turned the radio on and told Swan to find the right station. "I'll be right back as soon as I go to the bathroom," I said. I wanted to eavesdrop on Mama's call and I didn't want Swan to see me. If she did, she might tell.

The Everlasting Now

"Mayor Puckett?" I heard Mama say. "Serena Sayre, here. I hate to disturb you in the evening, but I have a problem. I need to talk to you about something that happened today between the sheriff and my son."

Oh, lordy, I thought. *She's gonna tell what happened and Lily's gonna find out and kill me.*

I went back to the parlor just as Fibber McGee's closet opened and everything fell out with a crash. Swan got tickled like she always does.

"I love him almost as much as I love Baby Snooks," she said.

* * *

On Sunday morning, Doc Phinizy was in the nave of First Presbyterian Church, giving out programs. I didn't take one 'cause I'm mad with him. After services, he and Mama walked out into the church yard and had a little talk. When she came back, Mama said he tried to explain what happened in his drugstore, and that he felt bad about it. But I don't care. He still ought to take that stupid sign down.

* * *

Early the next morning, I was in a hurry to get out of the house before Lily arrived, so I offered to go pick blackberries. Swan wanted to come too, but Mama said she'd get chiggers, so I went by myself.

Confederate and Union soldiers are buried in the old cemetery down the road. It's a good place with lots of shady trees so it's cool. The biggest blackberries and dew-berries grow there. The only problem is they grow in the hedges where there isn't much shade.

Picking blackberries is almost as bad as picking cotton, which I've never actually done, but it must be about the same. It's hot work, the bugs swarm around you, your fingers get pricked with thorns, and you have to watch out for snakes. If I hadn't been so scared of what Lily was going to say when she found out I'd squealed, I wouldn't have done it even for money. Which, by the way, I didn't get.

The sun was high by the time my pail was full so I decided to go home. I was too miserable to go anyplace else and besides, I didn't have any place to go.

Meadowlarks swooped over fields where tall grasses lapped in green waves. I walked up the grassy rise, climbed the split-rail fence, and went into the apple orchard. Only it's not really an orchard any more, just old trees that produce small, hard apples that Mama says are only good for cooking. Wild roses climbed their branches and wasps droned over windfall fruit.

When I came out on the other side of the orchard, Lily was standing at the clothesline, hanging out the wash. I tried to slip back into the shelter of the trees, but she'd already seen me. She glared at me, her face like a thunder-cloud.

"You're a fine piece of work," she said. "What'd I tell you?"

"Not to worry Mama," I said.

"Uh-huh. Didn't do much good, did it?"

Then I got kind of mad. After all, I was in the middle of what happened, too. "Lily," I said, "yesterday wasn't Champion's fault *or* mine."

"Brother," she said, "I love Champion, he's my blood. But there's things about living here that he doesn't understand. You either."

"I think I'm learning," I said, "and it stinks!"

"We have to live in this town, and we don't make the rules," said Lily.

"Does the sheriff?"

"Some of them," she said.

"He's got no right to do that!" I said.

"Coloreds don't *have* any rights, Brother. How come you haven't figured that out? If we get in trouble, we have to hope for help from somebody like your mama, and some of the other folks in town. Most of the time we just mind our business and keep our heads down.

"There's an old saying: 'As long as you got your hand in the lion's mouth, you have to be easy 'til you get it out.' You understand?"

Feeling worse every second, I just nodded, hoping that something would happen to stop my torture. Then, Lily reached into the clothes basket and began hanging sheets on the clothesline.

"Never mind," she said, "the damage is done. Take those berries inside and rinse 'em off in the sink. I think I'll make a cobbler for dessert."

Chapter Eleven

In late afternoon, dark thunderclouds began building in the west. Lily brought the clothes in, then left to go to the farm before the rain caught her. The sky was glassy, the air smelled of sulphur, and the birds grew quiet. Then rain began drifting across the fields in silvery sheets. Fat drops pocked the dust, flattening on the boards of the porch.

"Check the upstairs windows for me, Brother!" Mama called from the dining room.

Rain drummed heavily on the roof as I went from room to room, closing windows. I was on my way downstairs when I saw Sheriff Hamm standing at the front screened door. His shirt was wet and rain glistened on his polished boots.

I knew this was going to happen, I knew it! Once Mama made that call to the mayor, I was dead. I wanted to pretend I didn't see him and go back upstairs, but I couldn't. My stomach felt like it was going to fall out. There was a ringing in my ears.

The Everlasting Now

He peered through the screened door and saw me.

"Tell your mama I'm here," he said.

I didn't say anything. I just turned and went into the dining room. For a minute, I stood there looking at Mama. She was laying out a dress pattern on the dining room table. The thin tissue paper crinkled under her fingertips as she pinned the pattern to the material. Swan sat in a corner dressing her dolls from scraps of cloth light as summer butterflies.

"Mama," I whispered. I was so scared my voice sounded squeaky. "The sheriff's outside on the porch."

In the muted light from the windows, Mama's face was pale. "Have him come in," she said, "then you and Swan make yourselves scarce."

"I'm not gonna leave you alone with him," I told her.

"It'll be all right," she said.

Swan and I hid behind the hall door.

When he first went into the room, I heard him say he was sorry about upsetting her. *Sorry my foot,* I thought. *He didn't look like he was sorry.* I bet he only said it 'cause the mayor made him.

Then I couldn't make out any more words, just a kind of mumbling. A few minutes later he walked back down the hall and out to the porch. Mama didn't walk to the door with him, the way she did with regular company.

We waited a second, then we left our hiding place and watched as he left the porch and went down the steps. The rain had ended and the air was fresh and clean; steam rose from the ground. The sheriff stomped down the front path,

77

his boots crunching on the gravel. Then he walked toward the gate, brushing past the tea roses that tumbled over the front fence.

We followed him out to the yard, and Shirley Boligee followed us, lifting her paws delicately over the wet grass. Swan picked her up. When Sheriff Hamm reached the gate, Swan called out to him, her voice high and thin as a pennywhistle.

"You ol' bully," she said. "You ought not be mean to folks. It's bad manners!"

I was so shocked I couldn't move.

The sheriff stopped and turned to face us. His face grew red, and he puffed up like a toad. He glared at Swan, but she didn't waver. She held her ground, her skinny little legs trembling, her cat in her arms.

"Well, little missy," he said in a low voice, "that's a fine cat you've got there. Let's hope it's got nine lives like it's supposed to." Then he turned and opened the gate.

Waves of anger swept over me. Winds rushed through my head and the air around me turned black. Stepping in front of Swan, I grabbed a handful of wet clay. Kneading it into a hard clod, I took aim, threw it, and hit him smack in the middle of his fat back.

"That's for Champion!" I said. Then I grabbed Swan's hand and we ran back to the house and safety.

Mama was standing at the front door and saw me throw the clod. When the sheriff got in his car and left, she called me. "Come here, Brother," she said.

I could see she was upset. I tried to tell her that I didn't plan to throw the clod, it just happened, 'cause I was so mad.

"I understand that," she said. "But anger just produces anger. I think you need to calm down and stay close to home for a while."

"How long?" I asked.

"A week," she said.

I don't understand grown-ups, not even my mother. But I never said I was sorry for what I did, because I wasn't. It was worth it. I never pitched that good before in my life.

* * *

It was a long week. The whole time I was confined to the house I kept waiting for the sheriff to come back and arrest me, but he didn't. I kept a good lookout, though. If I saw him coming I was going to escape out the back. Lily kept giving me sideways looks. She said that Champion wasn't allowed to come to the house. I couldn't go fishing and when I asked her if Jesse and Champion had been, she just said, "I don't know what they're up to. Workin', I expect."

The railroad men didn't show up the whole time I was in prison. Then, at breakfast, Mama poured herself a cup of coffee and made her announcement.

"Your ordeal has ended," she said.

That same day, I was in the backyard weeding the flower beds. Not because I was still in trouble, but because Mama said they needed it. Swan was up in the chinaberry tree, singing at the top of her lungs:

Throw out the lifeline across the dark wa-a-ave,
There is a brother whom someone should sa-a-ave...
Somebody's brother! Oh who then, will dare
To throw out the lifeline, his peril to sha-a-a-are!

Every time she said the word "brother," she sang louder.

Champion came around the corner of the house. I was surprised to see him even though Mama and Lily had decided that he could come over. We weren't allowed to go to town or anyplace else where the sheriff or Mr. Linton might see us. It was too dangerous.

He waved to Swan, who was still singing.

"Don't let on like you hear her," I said. "She's just showing off. What've you been doing while I was in prison?"

"Moving pigs," he said.

I was surprised; he didn't like pigs any better than he did mules.

"Grandpapa was fixin' the pigpen," he explained. "So we had to put 'em in the shade so they wouldn't get sunstroke."

"Oh, so you had to move 'em." That made sense.

Swan started in on the chorus:

Throw out the lifeline!
Throw out the lifeline!
Someone is drifting awa-ay-ay-ay-ay-ay;
Throw out the lifeline!
Throw out the lifeline!
SOMEONE IS SINKING TODAAAAAY!

80

"Help me finish weeding," I said, "then let's get out of here. I'm going stir-crazy." After we finished the flower beds, we piled the weeds in the wheelbarrow and took them to the compost heap. That's when we decided to go down to the railroad tracks.

"Nobody'll bother us down there," I said. "Only don't tell Swan where we're going. She'll want to come, too."

I helped Swan down from the chinaberry tree. She told Champion that I'd been punished. "It wasn't fair," she said.

"Go tell Mama we'll be back in a little while," I said.

"Okay," she said. She picked up her cat and went inside.

As we sneaked out of the backyard, I told Champion why I'd been punished.

"You really hit the sheriff with a clod? All Aunt Lily told me was that you were in trouble and couldn't leave the house. And that I couldn't come see you."

I told him what the sheriff had said to Swan. "He was mean to her about her cat. It made me mad, him picking on a little girl. All of a sudden I was aiming for him."

"You did right. What'd Shirley Boligee ever do to him?"

"What'd *you* ever do to him?" I said.

"Brother," he said, "after you hit him, were you scared?"

"Naw," I said. But I told a lie. I was scared, I still am. I keep thinking about him and what he might do. "Mama said to give him a wide berth."

"What's that mean?" he asked.

"That's what I asked, and she said it means to stay as far away from him as I can. And I'd be glad to, only I never know when I'll see him."

After that, we called him all the bad names we knew. Champion knew more bad words than I did.

"I believe folks talk worse in Detroit than in Snow Hill," I said.

"Some do, some don't," he said.

Chapter Twelve

The railroad tracks smelled cindery in the hot sun. Dragonflies hovered over grass that was cut to stubble for the train's passage. If we'd had some pennies we'd have put them on the tracks for the train to flatten, but we didn't have any.

"Hey," said Champion, "know what we could do?"

"What?"

"We could hop a freight to Joe Louis's training camp!"

"Where is it?"

"New Jersey."

"New Jersey? Are you crazy? Why, that might just as well be France, or someplace."

"What do you know about France?" he asked.

"'I love Paris, I love France, where they don't wear no underpants,'" I sang.

Champion was laughing as he walked ahead of me down the tracks. Suddenly, he stopped stock-still, and I bumped into him.

A big colored man was stretched out on the side of the tracks, his hat sideways on his head. We eased over and stood looking down at him.

"Is he dead?" I whispered.

Suddenly, his big hand shot out and grabbed my ankle. I was so scared my eyes were watering. But when I tried to pull away, it was like I was caught in a vise. Looking through the mist, I saw Champion scrambling to get out of the way, but he was too slow. The man reached out and with his other hand grabbed Champion's ankle.

"Yiieeeks!" Champion hollered at the top of his lungs. You could've heard him yelling all the way to Boaz.

"Whoa! Hold on there," said the man, "I ain't gon' hurt you. Amos Ragsdale never hurt nobody."

* * *

For somebody who'd nearly scared us to death, Amos Ragsdale turned out to be a nice man. A hobo, he was on his way to Florida to pick fruit.

"Why were you laying by the tracks?" I asked. "We thought you were dead."

"I lay alongside so I can feel the train comin' a long way off," he explained. "You see, I been ridin' side-car Pullmans, what you call boxcars, for three years now. You gotta be careful, ridin' the rails."

I looked over at Champion, who ignored me.

"Some places," said Amos, "the law'll catch you and put you on a chain gang. Once, the railroad bulls took me off a train and arrested me for vagrancy. They called me a *vagrant!*"

"How old do you have to be for them to call you a vagrant?" I asked, thinking about being put on a chain gang.

"Old as they say," he answered. "So if you boys was thinkin' about ridin' the rails, think again."

Crows called over warm, empty fields that smelled of grass. The rails were hot to the touch and shone silvery in the sun. Amos wiped the sweat from his face with a red bandanna.

"Last time I got out of jail, they give me thirty-five cents and a pair of overalls. Bein' a hobo ain't all it's cracked up to be. Sometimes, you go hongry. There was one time, I knocked on folks' doors for food. Wouldn't nobody feed me."

"My mama would have," I said. "And Lily. They'd give you supper."

"So, you got a mama?" Amos asked.

"I do."

He looked at Champion. "You got a mama?"

"In Detroit," he replied, "but my Aunt Lily's here."

"She's the one you was speakin' of?" he asked me.

"The same one," I said.

"You boys get on home to your mama and your aunt," he said. "It ain't safe out here."

"Let's go," I said.

* * *

In late evening, chimney swifts darted and swooped over the treetops and the steady drone of crickets hummed on the warm air. Mama came downstairs dressed up in a white dress with red polka dots.

"Brother, you and Swan go get cleaned up, now. We're going to church this evening."

"I've been to church once this week," I said.

"Well, you can go again to hear Miss Eaton. She's a missionary who flew out of China in an American Volunteer Corps plane. Japanese troops were shooting at them. That took real courage. Just imagine!"

I'd have to imagine courage. I sure didn't have any. All I knew about was being scared.

"Is the pilot gonna be there too?" I asked.

"Of course not," said Mama.

"Then I don't want to go hear a missionary lady."

"It might do you some good," she said.

"Besides," I said, thinking of a good reason not to go, *The Shadow* comes on tonight. Lily already said Champion could come over if it's all right with you."

"I don't know, Brother. I'm not sure about leaving you two here alone."

"'Lamont Cranston will foil another horrifying plot!'" I said, putting my arm across my face like Dracula.

"I'll go with you, Mama," said Swan. "I don't like that spooky show. If I stayed home, Brother'd try to scare me."

"I would not!" Sometimes I wanted to pinch her hard as I could, but I knew better. "Nobody'll even know he's here," I said.

She finally gave in, and when Champion arrived, she told us the rules.

"If it rains, check the windows. Lock the doors when we leave and don't let anybody in. Turn on the porch light, so if anybody comes to the door, you'll know who it is. If it's a stranger, don't open it."

A little while later, the Maxwell crunched down the gravel drive and rumbled over the cattle gap. I had just turned on the radio when the telephone rang. By the time I finished telling Mrs. Holman where Mama had gone and why, it was time for our program.

Shadows cloaked the corners of the house. A single lamp burned in the hall. Candleflies searched out the rose-patterned light, flew too close, and fell onto the hall table.

In the parlor, the radio lights glowed soft gold. We wanted the room dark 'cause it made the program scarier. It was one time I liked being scared 'cause it wasn't real. I hadn't turned on the porch lights, but I would before Mama got home.

Champion sat cross-legged in front of the radio, holding Shirley Boligee in his arms. I lay down on the floor. Organ music swelled and filled the high-ceilinged room. Then a voice, low and menacing, whispered, *"Who knows what evil lurks in the hearts of men…? The Shadow knows."*

Shirley Boligee pricked up her ears and stared into the darkened hall. I hate it when cats do that, like they can see or hear something we can't. It gives me the creeps.

Then I heard something, too.

Creak…creak…creak… Footsteps moved stealthily across the floorboards of the porch.

I sat up. Champion looked at me, his eyes wide. Shirley leaped from his arms, her ears laid back, her body flattened as she slipped under the sofa, pulling her tail in after her.

There was a rasping noise at the front door—*scrabble, scrabble, scrabble*—like a rat scratching against a wall. I waited for a knock, but none came. The scratching grew more desperate, filling the hollows and dark places of the old house. I was pretty sure it wasn't a hobo; they always came to the back door, and never at night. We tiptoed over to the front window and, easing back the curtain, peeked out.

A figure stood in the shadows, his face hidden. A cloud passed over the moon. The porch grew dark and the figure became part of the darkness.

"I forgot to lock the door," I whispered.

"I did it," said Champion.

"And I didn't turn on the porch light. I was busy talking to Mrs. Holman."

The moon came out from behind the clouds. Our night visitor took shape, although his face was in shadow. But I knew him, even in the dark, I knew him. It was Mr. Linton.

"I saw him on my way over here!" said Champion. "He was goin' down the road in front of me. And he was walkin' funny."

"How could he know we're here?" I whispered.

"Maybe he saw the car leave," said Champion. "If he did, he'd figure we're here and Miss Serena isn't. Or maybe he watched me come up to the house."

The Everlasting Now

The scrabbling noise stopped and in the sudden silence, the hateful sound lingered like smoke. Footsteps moved toward the window. Easing up to the windowsill, I closed my eyes and braced myself to look out. My worst nightmare is looking into the dark and seeing someone, or something, looking back at me.

Taking a deep breath, I looked through the darkened glass. Deep hollow eyes stared back at me! I stumbled backwards, knocking the breath out of Champion, who was right behind me. He hit the floor like a sack of meal.

"Ooof!" he said, rolling over and getting to his knees.

For a minute, we just stayed on the floor. Then we heard him stumble back from the window. Peeking out again, we watched as he walked kind of lopsided over to the edge of the porch. He stood for a moment, weaving back and forth. Then, lurching down the steps, he wandered across the lawn.

We counted to ten, then eased down the front hall, staying close to the wall. The glass panels on the sides of the front door shone blackly.

"Ready?" I said, reaching for the door handle.

"Ready," whispered Champion.

The sweet, cloying scent of honeysuckle washed over us. We hid behind a column covered by the trembling leaves of wisteria and looked out into the yard. Only the leaves moved. Our night visitor was gone.

"He was drunk, wasn't he?" Champion said.

"Drunk and mean," I said.

We were sitting on the front steps. For some reason, we felt safer outside. Maybe because the house seemed so big and empty.

* * *

We heard the rumble of the cattle gap. "Get ready to run," I said, but then the lights of the Maxwell cut a swath through the night. Mama and Swan came up the walk.

"Why are you boys sitting out here in the dark? Did the power go off?"

"No, ma'am," I said.

"I bet they've been tryin' to scare each other," said Swan.

"No, we weren't," I said.

Champion looked over at me and nodded his head.

"I have something to tell you," I said.

"What? What happened?" Mama asked.

"Mr. Linton came by and kind of scratched on the door," I said. "But we didn't open it. I'm pretty sure he was drunk."

"I had a bad feeling about leaving y'all here alone," said Mama. "That sorry piece of work has no business coming by this house. I won't have it!"

Heat lightning lit up the sky like distant fireworks. The thin twanging of rain frogs rose and fell.

Champion got to his feet. "I best be goin' now," he said. "Aunt Lily might get worried."

I knew he was scared stiff to go out in the dark alone. I would be.

"We'll drive you home," said Mama, "it's not safe out with that man wandering around. Just let me go turn on some more lights and we'll go."

The Everlasting Now

* * *

After she heard Swan's prayers, Mama came and sat on my bed. The bedside lamp made a halo around her hair.

"You're not keeping something from me, are you?"

I laid my book down. "No, ma'am. I told you the truth. I'm pretty sure it was Mr. Linton, but I couldn't see his face too good."

Mama got up and adjusted the fan at the foot of my bed so it would rotate back and forth.

"You tell me if you do see him around here. And stay away from him. Pay attention to what's going on."

"I hope I don't ever see him again as long as I live."

Chapter Thirteen

Mama's book club was meeting at our house. The ladies met once a month at each other's houses to discuss a book one of them had just read. Whoever had the meeting served dessert and tea. Our house was the most popular because Lily made the best desserts in town.

"Go sweep the front porch for me, please," Mama said. "Our guests will be here soon."

The porch looked fine to me, but I didn't argue. Ladies seem to see things other folks don't. Shirley Boligee was asleep under one of the rocking chairs.

"You better get out from under there," I said, "before somebody rocks on your tail." But she just opened her eyes a slit, tucked her nose to her tail, and ignored me.

The ladies arrived and settled themselves in the parlor. Picking up the book I'd borrowed from Mr. Edwards, I decided to disappear. I tried to stay out of the way while the ladies were meeting. And while most of them are nice, I didn't want to be hugged or told how much I've grown. Swan acted cute, so she was welcome.

As I passed the door, I saw Mrs. Hartridge holding up a newspaper.

"Lord'a mercy, Serena," she said, her voice high and thin. "How come you're readin' this Yankee paper?"

"Captain Wooten brings it when he can," said Mama. "Mrs. Roosevelt's column, "My Day," is in it."

"Good grief," said Mrs. Hartridge.

I sat out on the front porch reading *Riders of the Purple Sage* 'til I heard the ladies getting ready to leave. Then I hurried around to the back. After lots of fluttery kisses and calling back and forth, they finally left.

I went into the kitchen, hoping there'd be some dessert left over. There weren't any leftovers in the icebox, so I checked the pantry. I couldn't believe my luck! A piece of blackberry pie, wrapped in waxed paper, was sitting there waiting for me. Just as I went back into the kitchen to get a fork, a hobo came walking up the back steps.

I quick slipped back into the pantry, leaving the door ajar so I could see. When he knocked on the screened door, Mama and Swan went to answer it.

"My name's Hopper," he said, his hat in his hand. His hair and beard were the color of a copper penny. "I was wonderin' if you could help me out with a bit of food, Missus. I don't have any money to pay, but if you'll allow, I could draw your little girl's picture. I'm a pretty fair artist," he said, taking a stick of charcoal from the pocket of his faded blue shirt. "And if you could see your way clear, maybe you could furnish me with a piece of paper?"

Something about him must have made Mama feel at ease. She told him to have a seat on the porch. Then she dished up a plate of black-eyed peas, sweet potatoes, and cornbread that Lily had cooked for tonight's supper. She handed the plate to Mr. Hopper, closed the screen door, and opened the pantry door.

"Brother, please fetch Mr. Hopper a glass of cool water." I swear, she's got eyes in the back of her head.

I took the glass out to the porch, then Swan and I sat with him while he ate his meal. He said he'd be glad of the company.

"You ever hear of the Federal Arts Project?" he asked, sopping up the juice from the peas with a bit of cornbread.

"Yessir," I said. "There's a mural at the post office that was painted by an artist with the FAP." I didn't tell him how silly the picture painted on the wall was—everybody grinning like a mule eatin' briars while they picked cotton in the heat.

"I'm hoping to get a job with them," Mr. Hopper said. "They'll hire me if I'm good enough. I'd like to paint a mural, too."

I thought, *if you know anything about cotton, you'd be good enough.*

He said that when he got out of art school, nobody was buying any art.

"I've got a friend working for the FAP. He got a job with them 'cause he couldn't make enough money to feed his family. Times are hard for writers and artists, harder than usual." He put his plate aside. It was so clean it looked like it had been washed.

"Some folks don't think much of artists; they think we're strange. One thing about the Depression though, with folks broke and unemployed, we don't seem so strange anymore."

Mama returned with some drawing paper, and a pad to work on, and Mr. Hopper started to draw Swan's portrait.

"Sit as still as you can," he said. And for once, she did as she was told.

"You don't look like a hobo, Mr. Hopper," she said, staring off into space.

"Shut up, Swan!" I said. "Don't be rude."

"It's all right, Brother," he said, making swift strokes with the stick of charcoal. "I am a hobo, for the time being. Do you know the difference between a hobo, a tramp, and a bum?"

"Nossir," I said.

"A hobo works and wanders. A tramp dreams and wanders. And a bum drinks and wanders."

Like Mr. Linton, I thought. He's a bum. It's kind of funny, but the homeless hobos I'd met were nice. It's some of the home folks that aren't.

In a little while, Mr. Hopper held up the finished drawing. One look and I knew the FAP would be lucky to get him. Swan took the picture inside to show Mama.

"Don't go yet, Mr. Hopper," I said. "I'll be right back."

I took him the pie, still wrapped in waxed paper. "It's

blackberry with a sugar crust. Our cook, Lily Luther, made it."

"Were you saving this for yourself, Brother?" he asked.

"Nossir," I said, crossing my fingers behind my back.

"I'm much obliged. I hope I can return the favor one day."

Mama thanked Mr. Hopper and put Swan's picture on top of the bookshelves that held some of Grandpapa Yeatman's law books. He was a brave man, even after he got death threats.

"The law's the law," he'd said, "and the person hasn't been born who can tell me how to defend it."

Hanging over the mantle under his portrait was the sword my great-grandfather carried in the Civil War. He was killed at Gettysburg. It seems like all the men in our family have been brave. Like my daddy, defending the picket line at the newspaper. If he were here, maybe he could teach me to be brave. As it is, I'm hoping to get braver as I get older.

Chapter Fourteen

The front hall was cool and quiet and smelled like beeswax. There was nobody downstairs, and the front door was open. Mama was out in the flower garden cutting roses and putting them in a basket.

"Your grandmother brought cuttings of this rose when she came here as a bride," she said. "It's a Madame Hardy." She bent her head over the white, open rose like she was drinking from a fountain.

Swan tiptoed across the dewy grass in her pajamas. "I can't find Shirley Boligee," she said. "I been lookin' for her, but I don't know where she is."

"She's probably playing tiger in the tall grass," said Mama. "She'll be back. Come on, let's get some breakfast. Did you remember we were going to a party today? Miss Martha Ward's niece is in town and she's having a tea party for her."

"Where's Lily?" Swan asked as we went back to the kitchen.

"It's Wednesday," said Mama. "She's taking the morning off instead of the afternoon."

At breakfast, Mama got up twice to go look for Shirley Boligee. Swan had checked Shirley's dish, but her food hadn't been touched. "She's never late to eat," said Swan.

When they were ready to go, and Swan was dressed up in her new pink dress and acting prissy, Mama stopped me in the hall. "Don't forget you need to go to the dairy. We don't need buttermilk, just some cream and a little butter. Take a couple of jars of Lily's pickled peaches with you. Adelaide just loves them. We'll be back later."

* * *

It was hot as a firecracker by the time I got back. My hat kept the sun off my head, but it didn't help much. I went in the back door and straight to the icebox. I put in the milk and butter, and poured a big glass of iced tea. But it was yesterday's and tasted like old wire.

Mama and Swan hadn't come back yet, and neither had Lily. I started to make a peanut butter and jelly sandwich, then I noticed that Shirley Boligee's food dish was still untouched. That wasn't right, so I went to look for her. I checked her favorite places in the house with no luck. She also likes to sleep in the shade of the climbing roses on the front porch.

"Well, there you are," I said when I saw her. Only she

wasn't in the shade; she was stretched out in a patch of sunlight on the top step. Her fur was dusty and sprinkled with bits of dried grass, like she'd been rolled in the weeds along the road.

When I touched her, she was too still. Then I saw the cord around her neck. Somebody had killed her.

Then it struck me that Mama and Swan could come back any minute! Swan couldn't see Shirley like this. I ran into the house and up the stairs to the linen closet. Grabbing the first sheet I could find, I raced back down to the porch.

Lily came down the front walk, carrying a basket of Indian peaches. When she saw me, she stopped for a second, then started running. The basket dropped from her hand; ripe peaches rolled across the ground like setting suns. Kneeling on the bottom step, she reached out her hand to Shirley.

"Do, Jesus," she said.

Taking all the care in the world, we wrapped Shirley in the sheet, then took her out to the pump house, where it's cool. She had to stay hidden 'til we could talk to Mama.

I picked up the peaches scattered over the lawn and took them into the kitchen. Lily was standing at the sink, crying.

"Don't cry, Lily," I said. "I can't stand it if you cry."

Wiping her eyes, she ran cold water over the peaches. Then she turned around and looked at me hard, like there was something written on my face. "Somebody did it on purpose," she said softly. "Somebody killed her and left her on the porch. It wasn't an accident."

I felt like my blood veins had turned to ice. Lily was right. And whoever killed her had planned it. They'd chased her and killed her. Then they'd waited 'til nobody was home, and left her for us to find. Words echoed in my head.

"Well, little missy, that's a fine cat you're got there. Let's hope it's got nine lives like it's supposed to."

* * *

Mama knew something was wrong the minute she saw us. She sent Swan upstairs to change her clothes. Then we told her about Shirley Boligee.

"Who would do something so wicked?" she said.

She kept the news from Swan until that evening. Then she told her that Shirley had died and was in heaven with the angels. Swan cried herself to sleep.

But I couldn't sleep. A whippoorwill called from the magnolia tree—*whip-poor-will...whip-poor-will...whip-poor-will*—the same call over and over again. It was making me crazy. Lily had said that if you tied a knot in the sheet, the bird would stop calling. I tried, but it didn't work.

* * *

The next day we had a funeral. Mama had brushed Shirley's fur and laid her in a tissue-filled shoebox.

Champion helped me dig a grave in the garden near

the sweet-shrub bushes. We found a smooth rock for a headstone, and Swan printed Shirley's name on it in blue paint. Jesse said a prayer at the graveside.

> *O Lord,*
> *Accept one of thy creatures into thy kingdom.*
> *Up beyond the evening star,*
> *out beyond the morning star,*
> *and where the angels sing.*

Afterwards, we had a "gathering," the way folks do when somebody dies. Only it was just us. Some people might say oh, it's just a cat, and not a person. But for us, it was the same thing. Shirley was part of the family, and whoever killed her broke Swan's heart. Ours, too.

We sat out on the veranda in the cool. Swan nibbled a cucumber sandwich with the crusts cut off. She was real quiet; she didn't talk or say how she was feeling.

Then, about dark when we were ready to go back inside, she finally spoke.

"Will Shirley Boligee have wings?"

"She surely will," said Mama.

"She'll fly all over God's heaven," said Lily.

* * *

The next few days passed slow as molasses. It was like walking in mud. Swan missed Shirley Boligee something terrible. Everybody moped around. Lily sang the blues, and Mama didn't sing at all. I didn't know you could miss a cat so much.

Jesse came by with a clutch of fresh eggs; they were all brown except for two. He had one hen that laid eggs blue as the sky and he brought those to Swan to make her feel better.

Chapter Fifteen

A few days after the funeral, Champion and I were sitting under the magnolia tree, where nobody could hear us. Katydids droned in the grass.

"I know the sheriff did it," I said. "I just know. Shirley likes...liked to play in the tall grass at the foot of the drive. I don't know how he caught her, maybe he had help. He didn't run over her, but he sure hit her. Mama thinks so too, now. Lily already did. But we didn't tell Swan."

"She's too little," said Champion.

"I just wish we could get even," I said. "We need to think of a plan."

"Yeah," he said, "and it better be a good one or he'll kill us, too."

That reminded me of Mama's announcement yesterday.

"From here on out," she said, "you and Champion aren't to go anyplace together where you might run into the sheriff. We know what he's capable of now, although we can't prove that he killed Shirley. It's not safe for you to be anywhere near him."

"I know what let's do," said Champion.

"About him?"

"No," he said. "We've got to think about that. This is something else but it's a good idea."

"I can't hardly think about anything else," I said.

"This will cheer you up," he said. "Let's go down to the creek and look for box turtles. I need me a pet that ain't a mule."

"We used to have a turtle that lived in the garden," I said. "When you gave him half an orange, he'd eat the sections clean as a whistle."

"If I had an orange, I'd eat it clean as a whistle, too," he said.

"C'mon," I said, getting up. "Let's look in the shed for a cardboard box to put him in."

"That's a good one," said Champion. "Box. Turtle. Get it?"

We walked down Old Post Road to the crossroads at Plantation Road. It's marked by a signpost, but it's covered in kudzu and sticks up in the ground like a green scarecrow. Out that way, kudzu vines rolled over everything in waves, covering trees, barns, and sheds, hiding them under thick, ruffled leaves.

Mr. Edwards said that kudzu grows so fast that sometimes he has to stop the train while workmen clear the tracks. In the fall, purple flowers bloom under the heart-shaped leaves and smell like grape soda.

The Everlasting Now

We turned down the narrow road leading to Thornhill Plantation and the creek. The plantation house had long disappeared; only tall columns mark the site where it used to stand. The woods were so green and still, it was like walking under water. We passed the old graveyard from the olden days. There's a spiky iron fence around it, and trees have grown up through the spikes. One sycamore tree looks like it swallowed part of the fence. Ancient tombstones lean into the earth, and moss grows over the words so you can't read anyone's name.

"This place is spooky," said Champion. "How far is the creek?"

"Not far now," I said. "You'll smell it in a minute."

"What's it smell like?" he asked.

"Kind of like iron," I said.

In a grove of willow trees, a crystal spring bubbled up from the ground and spread out into a wide creek that rippled and curled over smooth brown stones. In the leafy quiet, only the sounds of water and birdsong could be heard. We scouted the creek bed for a long time, but we didn't see a single turtle. I sat down at the creek's edge.

"You 'bout ready to go?" I said. "I'm gettin' hungry."

"Just a little bit longer," said Champion, moving to an outcropping of rocks jutting out into the water. A brown box turtle with bright yellow patches sunned itself on a flat rock.

"Bingo!" he whispered, pointing to the turtle.

We waded out quiet as we could but just as we reached the rock, the turtle plopped under the water and disappeared.

Long shadows fell through the woods. At the graveyard, the tombstones rose up, pale as ghosts in the greening light. A shadow passed along the fence like a phantom, moving from tombstone to tombstone. Along the roadside, willow trees trembled in a breeze that wasn't there.

We saw an old shed completely covered in kudzu. The thick vines had pressed down on the rickety roof like an open hand, squashing one side of it. The green cloak of leaves trembled lightly.

"What's that funny smell?" Champion asked, sniffing the air.

"I don't know. It's not the creek. Maybe it's something blooming. It stinks."

The closer we got to the shed, the stronger the smell; it was bitter and sweet at the same time. Then there was a kind of scraping sound that seemed to come from inside the shed, like something being pushed, or moved. The hairs on the back of my neck prickled. I had the feeling we were being watched.

We started walking fast, looking straight ahead. Something was out there, and whatever it was, I didn't want to see it. If I turned around and saw something scary, I might turn into a pillar of salt, like Lot's wife in the Bible.

Then we started running as fast as we could; Champion was way ahead. We reached the crossroads and headed out to the Old Post Road. A short distance from the crossroads, a black Ford sat hidden behind a tall clump of thick bushes.

* * *

The Everlasting Now

When I got home, Mama surprised me and told me we were going to a church supper that evening. I didn't have time to think up an excuse for not going, and I didn't think one would work anyway.

In town, sprinklers whirled and birds flew in and out of the water, ruffling their feathers. Children played hide-and-seek while the grown-ups sat out on their porches, taking the air.

The church supper was at the church hall. But before we ate, we had to listen to a guest speaker talk about missionaries in China and how they were suffering. I was suffering from hunger myself.

Finally, it was time to eat. I filled my plate with stuff I liked: fried chicken, peach cobbler, sweet-potato biscuits, and corn bread. I passed up the casseroles; you never know what's in them, might be squash or something worse.

By the time supper was over, the lights had come on at the softball field across the street. A high school softball game was being played. Mama said I could go watch, but not to go off anywhere else. I wandered over to the bleachers and saw Coach Spellman.

"Hey, Brother," he said. "How you been? Haven't seen hide nor hair of you. You doin' all right?"

I was glad to see him, and some of my friends from school. I guess I'd missed them without knowing that I had. And for a little while, as I watched the game, I didn't think about the watcher in the woods. I tried not to, anyway. About half an hour later, I went back over to the church.

It wasn't good dark yet, but people were leaving, while

others were standing out front talking and getting ready to leave. Mrs. Holman was looking after some little kids who were playing in the churchyard. Swan was sticking to her like glue. I went over to where Mama was talking to Mr. Holman.

"Hey, Brother," he said. "I was talking to Jesse's grandson about you."

"Champion? Where?"

"Well, everybody knows that Jesse Luther's got the best crop of 'gentlemen corn' of anybody around here, and I was out at his place buying a bushel. We were out in the yard when his grandson ran up to us like the very devil was after him.

"He told us he'd run through two pastures, dodged a bull, and climbed every fence along the way. When Jesse asked him why, he said he had to get off the road. That a man was chasin' him in a car!"

I heard Mama draw in her breath, but she didn't say anything.

"I asked him if he knew who it was, but he wouldn't say. 'Course he's just visiting, and might not know, but I got the feeling he was too *scared* to say. He did say that you two had been looking for box turtles down at the creek and saw something strange."

"We didn't really *see* anything," I said, "but we passed an old shed and something was there. The place smelled funny."

"I see," said Mr. Holman. "Well, about that time, who should ride up to the farm but the sheriff. I guess he was kinda surprised to see me, 'cause he backed that old Ford up, turned around, and went back the way he'd come."

"This has gone far enough," said Mama. "Something has to be done about that man."

"Let me look into it," said Mr. Holman. "And don't you fret about it."

Chapter Sixteen

I wish Lily had a telephone," I said.

"I expect she does, too," said Mama. "A lot of folks would like to have one, but they don't."

"Well, I think I'll go over to the farm," I said.

"No," said Mama, "not this morning. Lily said they had plans for today and they're busy over there. You stay here. If you're bored, I can find something for you to do. You can read 'Peter Painter' to your sister."

"Peter Painter" was a series of stories in one of the newspapers that Captain Wooten saved for us. Ol' Peter was a goofy fairy who flew around painting leaves in the fall. The stories were horrible but Swan loved them. She could read 'em herself, but she likes for other people to read to her.

"I'll find something to do," I said.

The Everlasting Now

I went out to the veranda to work on a jigsaw puzzle that Mr. Edwards had brought that had five hundred tiny pieces and showed a train pulling into a big city station. After a while, I got tired of it and went upstairs to my room. I pulled my cigar box out from under the bed. There wasn't much in it: a pack of baseball cards, an Indian Head penny, and some really fine agates. Then I read a chapter of *Code of the West*, by Zane Grey. If we had a "Code of the West" in the South, the sheriff would be done for, I thought. Somebody ought to string him up.

* * *

The next morning, I was still in bed when Swan pulled at my big toe. When I opened my eyes, the room was gray, like fog.

"Mama's gone and it's rainin'," she said.

"Gone where?"

"I don't know. She said I couldn't go with her, and not to wake you up."

"Come on," I said, getting out of bed, "let's get some breakfast."

"I'd rather wait for Lily. She's the only one can fix good breakfast."

But Lily never showed up. I had a funny feeling in my stomach, like when you know something's going to happen, but you don't know what.

A rainstorm had blown in overnight. I looked out of the window at the front garden. It looked like an underwater

111

world; flowers and bushes waved in a gentle tide. Rainwater gushed from the eaves of the porch.

Splat! A tree frog landed on the windowpane. He was green as grass, his pink toe pads like tiny suction cups. Seen through the wavy old glass, he was fuzzy and out of focus.

Swan was making a doll house on the bottom step in the hall. Her paper dolls were cut out from old pattern books, so they had lots of clothes. She dressed one and sat her at the tiny table.

"When's Mama comin' back?" she said. "I'm hungry."

"You had cereal," I said. "Now leave me alone. I'm thinking."

"Wheaties are for boys, so they can be champions," she said. "I only like Raisin Bran. Besides, it's almost time for dinner."

The Maxwell swept up the drive, its headlights gleaming through the rain. Mama walked up on the porch, shook the rain from her umbrella, and came into the hall. Hanging her raincoat on the hall tree, she pulled off her black rubber galoshes and held them up. "These old things leak," she said. "You suppose we could patch 'em, like inner tubes?"

"Where'd you go?" I asked.

"To Lily's," she replied.

"Is she sick?" I asked. "You were gone a long time."

She shook her head. "No, she's not sick."

At the foot of the stairs, she stopped to admire Swan's doll house. "Are those acorn tops for cups? And you're using buttons for plates. You are so clever, darlin'." Mama was talking too fast, like she was in a big hurry or something.

"Brother made me eat Wheaties," said Swan.

* * *

The next day I learned what the bad thing was that I felt, but didn't know. When I went down for breakfast, Mama and Lily were sitting at the kitchen table, drinking coffee. They were talking kind of whispery. When I walked in, they looked like I'd surprised them. I poured cereal in a bowl and sat down at the table.

"There's something we have to tell you," Mama said, "about yesterday. You know when you wanted to go over to the farm?"

"Yes, ma'am," I said. I knew she was going to say something I didn't want to hear.

"We took Champion to the bus station."

"We don't have a bus station," I said, pouring milk on my cereal. "All we have's a filling station."

"To the bus station in Selma," she explained, "so he could go back to Detroit."

"Go back? What do you mean, go back? Why?"

"We had to get Champion out of town. He was in danger here. The best thing was to send him home. The only thing that saved Champion the other day was that Mr. Holman was out at Jesse's farm when the sheriff showed up. It's plain that he was after him."

"He'd have got to Champion one of these days," said Lily.

"Papa decided that the best thing was to send him home."

"We had to get him away from here and we had to do it secretly," said Mama.

"I didn't even get to tell him good-bye," I said, pushing the cereal bowl away. I wasn't hungry anymore.

Swan came in and sat at the table. Looking around, she said, "Why's everybody sad?"

Lily told her that Champion had to go home. Then she said, "Come on, sweet girl, help me make the toast."

Mama explained why they were busy the day I'd wanted to go over to the farm.

"Jesse didn't have enough money for a bus ticket, and for some extra to send to Rose. He had to borrow some from Mr. Tamplin at the hardware store. After the bank closed, he started lending money to local farmers. Not big money, but enough to help them out 'til their crops come in," said Mama.

"Papa took out a mortgage on Nicodemus," said Lily, putting a jar of blackberry jelly on the table.

"I don't know what that means," I said.

"It means that if Papa's fall crops fail, he could lose Nicodemus," she said, "and he loves that old mule." She held out her hand to me. "Come with me. There's something you need to see."

In the parlor, sunlight slipped through the blinds, sheening the top of the Grundig console in golden dust. On top of it, Joe Louis in a bottle glittered in the light.

"Champion wants you to keep it 'til he gets back," said Lily.

But nobody knew when that would be, if ever.

The Everlasting Now

I took Joe Louis in a bottle out to the front porch. The garden sparkled with yesterday's rain, and mockingbirds searched for worms in the wet grass. In a little while, Swan came and sat beside me in the swing. She pressed her forehead against the glass of the demijohn like she was looking into an aquarium.

"Who's that man in the middle?" she asked.

"Joe Louis," I said. "He's a boxer."

"Will Champion ever come back?" she asked, kicking her legs to rock the swing.

"I don't know." For the life of me, I couldn't understand how grown men could hate a kid because he's colored. Or why they hated me 'cause we were friends.

"Maybe he can come back when the mortgage goes away," Swan said.

I tried to explain. "A mortgage is when you borrow money on something you own. You have to promise to pay it back, or you lose what you owned. It's like a trade. I guess the only thing Jesse has that's worth anything is his mule. It's funny, Champion didn't even *like* Nicodemus. But that old mule maybe saved him from something bad."

"How'd Champion get those little flags in the jar?" Swan asked.

"I don't know."

"Poor old Nicodemus," she said, "havin' to carry a mortgage around all the time."

There was no use explaining any more. I didn't much understand it either.

"I'd like to know who made up all the rules around here," I said.

"What rules?"

"The ones that say what some people can do, and some can't. The rule that says coloreds can't play on the same team as whites, even if they're good players. The rule that says coloreds have to sit in the balcony at the picture show. And the rule that says they can't sit at the drugstore counter. I hate that damn ol' rule!"

"You said a bad word!" said Swan. "I'm tellin'."

"I don't care. Everything's spoiled anyway."

But she didn't tell.

Chapter Seventeen

I was glad that the railroad men were finally coming back. "Seems like a long time since they've been here," I said.

"Sure does," said Mama, wiping the rocking chairs with a damp cloth.

I was getting ready to go to the dairy when Mr. Holman's old pickup truck wheezed and rattled its way up the drive. He got out and came up the front steps.

"Adelaide's sent a little surprise for Swan," he said. "So I figured I'd drop the buttermilk off at the same time, save Brother a trip." He handed me the milk and set a cardboard box down on the porch.

"I need to talk to you for a minute, Serena," he said.

"Have a seat," said Mama.

As I started back to the kitchen with the buttermilk, he said, "If it's all right with you, Serena, Brother might like to hear what I've got to say."

I knew it had to be serious. I wondered if I'd done something wrong.

"Pour us some iced tea while you're in the kitchen," said Mama, "then come on back."

Mr. Holman started talking about the day he was at Jesse's farm. "Champion told Jesse and me where you boys had been. No harm in that. I couldn't figure out why the sheriff was so all-fired bent on coming after him. It didn't make sense—unless the sheriff had something to hide. So I decided to see what all the fuss was about." He took a swallow of iced tea and continued.

"I drove out to the woods near Plantation Creek. And guess what I found?"

"What?" I asked.

"A moonshine still! Some fool had been making whiskey, and must have got scared that you two had stumbled onto it. I knew there wasn't any point in calling the sheriff's office, so I drove to town to tell the mayor. But by the time we got some help and went back, the still was gone. Nothin' left but a bad smell and some old copper tubing. You could see where it had been set up in the old shed, but it had been moved— lock, stock, and barrel!"

"Was that what we smelled?" I asked. "The still?"

"You smelled the likker in it," he said. "That stuff'll make you blind."

"Lonnie," said Mama, "you are a hero. We'd put your picture on the front page of the newspaper if we still had one."

Something shifted in the cardboard carton; two dark, fuzzy ears stuck up from the box like bat's ears.

118

Swan heard us and came out onto the porch, holding her Raggedy Ann doll by one leg.

"Hey, Mr. Holman," she said, eyeing the box.

"Come see what he's brought," said Mama.

Swan looked into the box, picked up the gray-striped kitten with the bat ears, and gazed into its heart-shaped face.

"Oh," she said, "the beautiful thing. Can I keep her?"

"Our barn cat had kittens 'bout six weeks ago," said Mr. Holman. "This one's the pick of the litter."

"What'd the others look like?" I asked.

Mama gave me a warning look.

"'Bout the same," he said.

"You'll have to think of a good name for the new kitten," said Mama.

"I'll think of a delicious name for her," said Swan, cuddling the scrawny kitten in her arms.

"It's a tom," said Mr. Holman. "You'll have to give it a boy's name."

"I'll think hard on it," she said, hugging its neck.

As he was leaving, he said, "Since the railroad men will be here this evenin', I'd like to pay them a visit."

"Come have dessert with us," said Mama. "Ask Adelaide to come, too. I haven't seen her since the church supper."

* * *

Mr. Edwards brought the train in at late afternoon. Lily had left their supper: fried chicken, corn pudding, and extra biscuits for Dusty.

At the supper table, Mr. Edwards asked the blessing. "The things, good Lord, that we pray for, give us the grace to labor for. Amen."

Swan piped up, "And bless Shirley Boligee in heaven, and Champion, and poor old Nicodemus."

Bowls and platters were passed down the table and the men filled their plates.

"I don't believe I know Nicodemus," said Dusty.

"He's a mortgage mule," said Swan.

After supper, the men went out to the veranda. I went with them.

"Come explain a mystery for us, Brother," said Mr. Edwards. "Just why was Swan praying for everybody, including a cat and a mule?"

Mama had warned me about bothering them with our troubles, but I couldn't help it. I had to tell how the sheriff had scared Swan about her cat. And about Shirley Boligee being killed. And I told them that Champion had to go back to Detroit because the sheriff was after him.

"It wasn't even time for him to go back," I said. "And Jesse had to take out a mortgage on his mule Nicodemus, to get some money."

"No man worth his salt picks on women and children or mistreats animals," said Dusty. His voice was soft but there was anger in it.

Mr. Holman's old truck rattled up the drive and a few minutes later, Mama led him out to the veranda.

"Adelaide said to thank you for the invitation, Serena, but she had to go see to her sister Lissie, who's feeling poorly. I'll pick her up on my way home."

Then Mama told me to come help her in the kitchen.

She put the bowls of peach cobbler on a tray with napkins and spoons. "You can take the tray in," she said, "then come back. Let the men talk in private. They might have business to discuss."

About dusk, Mr. Holman said his good-byes. Swan followed him out to the front porch in her pajamas, her new kitten in her arms.

"I decided on a name," she said. "I'm naming him after granddaddy and Tarzan. His name's Judge Tarzan."

"That's a fine name," said Mr. Holman. "I'll be sure to tell my wife."

Everybody just called the kitten Judge.

Chapter Eighteen

In August, we got hit by a heat wave that was plain awful. It was so hot you could've fried an egg on a sidewalk, only nobody wanted to waste an egg. Sparrows took dust baths in the garden, and rain frogs begged for rain. Mama kept the sprinklers on in the yard so the birds could get some relief. Most folks just hunkered down in the heat. Even the hobos were staying put. It was so hot I didn't even have to cut the grass. Besides, it wasn't green anymore, just dry and brown.

There wasn't much to do, so I went down to the depot to see if anything was going on down there. I didn't figure there'd be much going on, though. The men had left before dawn that morning. But Mama said I couldn't see them off at that hour. "You don't need to be getting up that early, not when it's still dark."

Lucius was sitting on the depot steps eating boiled peanuts. Across the tracks, locusts thrummed in the fields, and meadowlarks had their fill of them. There was a strong smell of creosote in the day's heat, and the flowers in the depot garden looked like they were worn out.

"Hey, Lucius," I said. "Whatcha doin'?"

"Hey, Bwowa," he said, offering me the wet bag of peanuts. "I got a job, woking for the wailwoad."

"Since when?" I asked. I wasn't really sure if he really had a job, or if he just thought he had.

"Today," he said, sucking a peanut out of the shell, then spitting the soft hull on the ground. "The shuff's done gone on the twain."

"Sheriff Hamm? What do you mean? What train?"

The only train that left the station that day was the freight train from Snow Hill for Montgomery early that morning.

"Lucius, there's no passengers on a freight train. Did you see the sheriff get on the train?"

"Uh-huh."

Now, ol' Lucius might be slow, but he knew about trains. He met every one that stopped in Snow Hill. And he greeted the express trains that slowed to pick up mail. He couldn't read the schedules, but he knew them by heart. And he wasn't likely to make a mistake about who he'd seen. He'd recognize the sheriff. That man had spent a lot of time making life miserable for Lucius and for anybody else that couldn't fight back.

"How 'bout a Co-cola, Lucius?"

I had two nickels 'cause I got paid to clean up the compost heap, which was an awful job. But I figured it was worth spending my hard-earned money to hear Lucius's story.

Dropping the nickels in the slot of the red Coca-Cola box, I sloshed my hand around in the icy water for two cold, green bottles. I opened them and handed one to Lucius. What he'd said was too good to be true, but I wanted to know.

"Tell me what you saw," I said.

Lucius screwed up his face and closed his eyes. Then, in between slow sips of his Co-cola, he told what happened.

He'd been sleeping in a boxcar on the siding when the door slid open, and a flashlight's beam searched the car.

"You get on up now, Lucius," a man had said. "We need to move this car to the train."

"Who was it?" I asked.

Lucius shrugged. "He had on a suit."

Conductors wear suits, I thought, *and they're in charge of the trains. They decide when to add boxcars or not.*

"Then what happened?" I asked.

"He gave me money for bwekfast and I got out," said Lucius.

A locomotive thrummed on the tracks, ready to go. High up on the engine, the headlight cut a swath through the early morning mists. Rising steam hid the stars. The freight train was bound for Montgomery, then on to New Orleans. There, it would be coupled to a train headed for Michigan, on the Canadian border.

Lucius said he watched as the conductor signaled to the flagman. Then the flagman, his lantern swinging in a

124

golden arc, checked the couplings on the boxcar.

"The door opened, and two mens went inside. In a little while, one came out by hisself."

Down the tracks, signal lights burned green. The stationmaster stepped out onto the platform.

"Gween!" said Lucius. "The lights was gween!"

The train left the station and clattered down the silvery tracks at dawn.

I sat on the steps, thinking. *Had the sheriff been put on the train? Why would he go?*

"Lucius," I said, "cross your heart and hope to die that it was Sheriff Hamm on that train."

He crossed his heart and drained the last of his Co-cola.

Could it be true? Was the fat ol' poop really gone? Maybe miracles do happen. 'Course he could come back—but maybe he wouldn't. Even if he was just gone for a while, it'd be great.

I felt like some giant hand had just wiped things away, and there was an end to the bad stuff. I took a deep breath; the smell of cinders, dust, and dry grass was so fine I thought I'd pass out.

"What a great day!" I said.

"I still needs me a hat," said Lucius, "now I'm wokin'."

I looked at his do-funny hair and wrinkled clothes. Something caught at my heart. "Lucius, how'd you like to have my daddy's best Dunlop hat?"

He frowned like he thought I was making fun, but I wasn't. I took it off and handed it to him. "I'm making you a present of it."

He stood up, balancing himself with his crutch. Taking the hat, he rubbed his fingers along the soft, felt brim. Then he put it on and tilted it the way Daddy had.

"Lucius thanks you," he said.

Chapter Nineteen

Sheriff Hamm was gone. In Snow Hill, the grapevine got the word out quicker than the telephone lines. The news was all over town; the sheriff had quit his job and left. Nobody was sorry.

"Good riddance to bad rubbish," Mama said when she heard the news.

"You reap what you sow," said Lily.

Mayor Puckett got a postcard from Michigan. The sheriff officially resigned "on account of health reasons," he wrote. He wouldn't be coming back. The mayor hired a new sheriff. Folks said he was bound to be better than the last one.

After a while, when she was sure in her mind that Sheriff Hamm wasn't coming back, Lily wrote a letter to Rose to let Champion know that he'd gone.

I never said a word about what Lucius told me. He doesn't always get things straight, but I believed his story about the train taking the sheriff away from here.

For the first time since I'd been picking up the mail and going to the library, I did it backwards. I went by the library first, instead of putting it off like I used to, when Sheriff Hamm was in town and I was afraid I'd run into him.

Miss Eulalie gave me a new book for Mama.

"*Lost Horizon*, by James Hilton," she said, closing her eyes blissfully. "It's so wonderful!"

Ah ha! I thought. Miss Eulalie reads the books first, just like Mr. Bartram reads postcards before he gives them to you.

Then I went to the post office. I was hoping for a postcard from Champion, but I didn't get one. When I looked through the mail, the only card was for Mama. A plant nursery in Evergreen was closing.

"Something else gone because of the Depression," said Mr. Bartram. "By the way, Brother, speaking of things gone. What happened to your hat? I hardly recognized you with hair."

"The hat's gone too," I said.

"Been to the courthouse lately?" he asked. "They're gettin' a new mural."

"It's not about cotton, is it?"

"Nope. Looks like it's gonna be a good one, real lifelike."

Footsteps sounded behind me. *Tippy-tap...tippy-tap...tippy-tap...* Miz Edna Earl was on the prowl.

"You might want to hurry on over and take a look," he said.

"Thank you, sir," I said, making my escape.

The Everlasting Now

*** *** ***

The courthouse had been built before the Civil War. Now the government was restoring it as a WPA project to put people to work. Mama said the real name was the Works Progress Administration, only everybody calls it the WPA.

"President Roosevelt started it, "she said, "to put the unemployed back to work. He said that when you give people jobs, it gives them back their self-respect, courage, and determination."

And it was working, at least around here. At the courthouse, workmen climbed over scaffolding that had been placed against the crumbling brick walls. Some were spreading new mortar to bind old bricks and other worked at moving supplies and tools. They were a busy lot.

In the cool vaulted lobby, marble columns rose to the second floor, their tops lost in shadow. There was a musty smell of old books, and the keen-edged odor of turpentine. Grandfather Yeatman's law office used to be upstairs, but somebody else had it now.

A man stood on a tall ladder against one wall. His overalls were smeared with paint, and there was a streak of white paint in his red beard.

"Mr. Hopper?"

"Why, it's Brother Sayre," he said. He climbed down the ladder and, wiping his hands on his paint cloth, held out his hand.

"It's good to see you," he said. "As you can tell, I got a job as an artist with the government. It sure saved my bacon." He gestured toward the wall, where I could see the outline of a mural.

"'Course, what's up there now is just the template; it's like a blueprint. I'll fill in the details later."

He'd drawn regular people—farmers and coal miners, railroad men, firemen, policemen, ladies in aprons and some in church hats.

"Come have a seat and catch me up on everything," he said.

We sat on one of the benches along the wall. He asked about Mama and Swan.

"They're fine," I said. "Mama framed Swan's picture that you drew. She's real proud of it."

He took his lunch pail from under the bench and offered me a sandwich.

"No sir, I can't," I said. "I have to get home. I just came to the library and to pick up the mail. At the post office, Mr. Bartram told me about the mural."

"I've been travelin' this land to get ready to paint," he said. "In West Virginia, I went down into a coal mine to see what it's like. The only way to tell between fair air and foul is if the canary dies. It's a hard way to make a living."

He poured tea from his thermos, then took a swallow.

"I picked fruit down in Florida and that was bad, too. They put you up in shacks so rotten, you'd be better off outside, except for rain. The mosquitoes get you anyway."

I was enjoying his stories when something happened. The tippy-tapping of heels clacked on the marble floor. Twice in one day was too much for me.

"Mr. Hopper, if I was you, I'd get back up the ladder. Miz Edna Earl's gonna want you to board with her, now that you've got a job."

But she got to us before he could get away.

"Well, James," she said to me, "I hope you're not trying to get this gentleman to come board at your house."

"I've been to his house, ma'am," said Mr. Hopper.

"Oh?" she said. "It was my understanding that you've just come to town. Did you stay with the Sayres before?"

"No, ma'am. When I was here before, I was a hobo. I was hungry and they fed me."

Her jaw dropped and she gave me a dirty look. "Well, I never!" she said, and flounced off. *Tippy-tap...tippy-tap...tippy-tap.*

Mr. Hopper closed his lunch pail and set it back under the bench. "That's payback for the blackberry pie, and your mama's kindness," he said.

When I got home, I told Mama about him maybe needing a room.

"But he didn't ask," I said. It made me feel good to think about him getting the best of Miz Edna Earl.

"We're pretty full up," said Mama. "But you could give up your room and share with Swan."

"I like Mr. Hopper," I said, "but not that much."

Chapter Twenty

The train whistle echoing over the fields sounded as sweet as the angel Gabriel blowing his horn. It had been a while since the railroad men had been here. But they'd barely walked in our door when folks began dropping by the house. Jesse was the first to come by. He was wearing his preacher clothes and had brought fresh-caught catfish, skillet corn bread, and two jars of pickled okra to go with the fish. He shook hands with the men and welcomed them back. Then the piano lady from his church came over with a big bowl of sweet-potato salad and a pot of turnip greens.

"I don't try to beat Lily at desserts," she told Mama, "but my vegetables are famous."

More church ladies showed up with good things to eat. By late afternoon, the icebox was stuffed with food. Bowls and casseroles lined the kitchen counters and the sideboard in the dining room held platters of chicken, ham, and small fried fish called scrompers. Jesse's church wasn't very big, but Mama said that's where the best cooks in town went to church. Swan skittered around like a butterfly, trying to see everything and generally getting in the way.

"I don't know what to think," said Mama, trying to find room for a basket of ham biscuits on the dining room table. "This is the kind of caring you get when a loved one dies, and folks bring food and gather around. Only everybody who came by just said how glad they were that the railroad men had come back."

"Just accept the bounty," said Lily, checking the bit of tape on the bottom of a plate to see who'd brought it. "I thought these buttermilk pralines were Hattie's. She does make the best."

"Who's she?" I said, reaching for a piece of the crisp, golden candy.

"She's one of my Five Golden Stars Minus One," said Lily, "and don't eat any more."

"Lily," I whispered, "did you invite the ladies from your church to come over today?"

"Brother," she said, "let's you and me step out to the porch for a minute.

"I didn't have to invite them," she said. "You have to understand that we have our own way of learning about things. Between the Pullman porters and the folks at the colored boardinghouse where they stay, and the ladies at our church who work for white people in white kitchens, there's not much we coloreds *don't* know. We've got a grapevine that's a heap better than the telephone lines."

Lily knew. She knew how the sheriff had disappeared, and a lot of folks in the black community knew as well. But it would be a well-kept secret.

"Brother," she said, giving me a hawk look. "You'd best stay honest. 'Cause everything you're thinkin' shows on your face."

Mama called and invited the Holmans for supper. Mr. Holman offered to pick up Miss Eulalie. That night's supper was the biggest and the best we ever had at our house. It was like a celebration.

* * *

In the early morning, Dusty was working on the Maxwell. I was sitting on the running board, watching him.

"This car's held together with spit and baling wire," he said. He thwacked the radiator lightly and adjusted the wires leading from the distributor. Then, like a master craftsman, he finished up by polishing the engine with a soft rag.

"Okay," he said. "Now try her, Brother."

I climbed into the driver's seat and turned on the engine. The car shuddered slightly, gave a little cough, and began to purr like a kitten.

"You did it!" I said. "I'm gonna ask Mama if I can take it down the drive."

The answer was "no."

"Maybe next time," said Dusty.

"Maybe," I said, but I didn't hold out much hope. I

probably wouldn't get to drive the car 'til I was twenty years old or more. By then, the danged thing might be up on blocks.

"How 'bout if we take her for a spin?" Dusty offered. "Just to be sure she's runnin' okay."

I climbed into the passenger seat. Swan came out and jumped down the front steps.

"Wait for me!" she called. "I want to go where you're goin'."

As we drove past the Holman's dairy, Swan called from the open window, "Thank you, Mr. Holman, for Judge Tarzan!"

"You surely got a fine cat," said Dusty.

We passed the sharecroppers' houses—old shanties sitting out in the fields. In the baked-earth yard at one house, two little boys were rolling around in the dirt.

"Don't they have any toys?" Swan asked as we went by.

The other houses looked empty, but it was hard to tell unless there was washing on the lines. Seems like they didn't ever hang curtains on the windows.

At Sammy's old house, the front door was half-open, hanging on its hinges. I could tell it was empty.

"Mr. Holman said they left in the middle of the night," I said. "Soon after he found that still in the woods."

"Is that a fact?" said Dusty. "I don't expect anybody will miss 'em."

"I expect not," I said, "except for Sammy."

In August, this season was about over. They'd probably moved to another house for another season. I was sorry about Sammy leaving. But I sure was glad I didn't have to think about that mean, skinny old man anymore.

* * *

On Sunday afternoon, the railroad men and I were sitting on the front porch after dinner. Captain Wooten was asleep in a rocking chair, and Dusty dozed behind the funny papers. Mr. Edwards was the only one awake, except me. He was reading the sports pages of the *St. Louis Dispatch* that the captain had saved for us.

"Listen to this, Brother," he said. "'Joe Louis and his softball team, The Brown Bombers, plan a special railroad trip to the South. Louis has requested a special car to be added to the train for his team.'"

"I thought I knew all about Joe Louis," I said. "But I didn't know he had a softball team."

"Yep," said Mr. Edwards. "They're a twenty-two member team made up of Joe's friends. Like most coloreds, they were out of work, even in Detroit."

"Twenty-two members," I said. "Guess they were lucky."

Mr. Edwards smiled. "I'd say Joe Louis was lucky to have twenty-two friends."

"I guess," I said.

Mr. Edwards kept reading. "It says here that the itinerary for the games hasn't been announced."

"What's an i-tin-er-ary?" I asked.

"It means the schedule," he said. "I guess they aren't sure just where the team will play, in which towns."

The Everlasting Now

"You reckon they'll come to Snow Hill? It's close to where Joe Louis was born. Gosh, that'd be somethin'!"

"I doubt it," said Mr. Edwards. "The train might come through here, but only on the way to a big town where they'd have a game. But we'll keep an ear out, you never know."

I knew.

There wasn't a chance. I wished he hadn't even told me about it.

Chapter Twenty-One

I was sitting in the parlor reading *Rightway Magazine*, the railroad newspaper, when Mama came in with her sewing box. She was making a school dress for Swan. The hour of doom was at hand. School would be starting in two weeks.

I showed her a drawing of a Mikado-type engine from the paper. "It says here, it was drawn by Jim Newman Jr., a colored section laborer. All he had to work with was a five-cent box of crayons and a ruler."

"He had more than that," she said, admiring the picture. "He had talent."

"This makes two artists I know about," I said. "Mr. Hopper is the other one."

"Brother, sit under the lamp if you're going to read. You'll ruin your eyes, holding that paper so close."

She turned on the radio to listen to the news. The floor

fan rustled the pages of the paper and droned on the warm air. White moths hit the screens, and a mourning dove called plaintively from the garden.

When the news was over, Mama folded up her sewing and rose to go. "It seems the Duke of Windsor got married," she said.

"Who's he?" I asked.

"He used to be the King of England. Now his brother, George Sixth, is king."

"I'd like to be a king," I said, thinking of King Arthur. "So if you stop being a king, you get to be a duke?" I knew about Duke Ellington, but he wasn't a real duke.

"No," said Mama, "that's not how it works. The Duke of Windsor abdicated, he resigned. He stopped wanting to be the king."

"Boy, that's dumb," I said. "Why'd he quit?"

"He married a woman from Baltimore," she said.

"That's like leaving rooms over the depot to go live with Miz Edna Earl," I said.

"Brother, sometimes you surprise me," said Mama.

* * *

The next day, there was a shout from the front hall. "Brother!" Lily yelled. "Come talk to Lucius. I don't know what he wants."

"Hey, Lucius," I said, going to the door. "What do you want?"

Taking off his hat, Lucius removed a telegram and handed it to me. I couldn't believe my eyes; it had my name on it. I stood there holding the yellow envelope.

"Mama!" I called, "come quick!"

Swan came too, and for a minute or so, we all stood at the door. It didn't occur to any of us that a telegram could be good news.

"Go on, open it," said Mama.

Very carefully, I opened the envelope and read the message aloud.

JOE LOUIS AND TEAM ARRIVING SNOW HILL STOP SPECIAL TRAIN LABOR DAY STOP DETAILS TO FOLLOW STOP
——E. L. EDWARDS, ENGINEER

Lily grabbed me so hard she nearly squeezed my guts out. Swan jumped up and down, and Mama went to get a tip for Lucius. When she handed him a nickel, he thanked her, put his hat back on, and limped back down the steps.

"I guess he is working for the railroad," I said.

When we'd all calmed down, we sat on the porch drinking iced tea.

"I'm gonna frame this telegram," I said.

"Brother," Mama said, "did Lucius's hat look familiar to you?"

"Yes, ma'am," I said.

* * *

The Everlasting Now

The details about the upcoming visit of Joe Louis and his softball team did follow shortly.

Mr. Edwards was the engineer on *The Joe Louis Special.* His softball team, The Brown Bombers, had been playing benefit games across the South. After a visit to the county where he used to live, Joe planned a brief stop at Snow Hill. The time was short, and there wouldn't be a softball game, but we'd get to see Joe Louis and his team.

When folks heard about the visit, they went kind of crazy. Nobody famous had ever come to Snow Hill, not even the governor. When Mayor Puckett learned that I got the telegram, he came to our house.

"We should have a Labor Day celebration," he said, beaming. "I'll oversee the whole thing."

At first, plans were made for two celebrations—one for whites, and one for coloreds. But since there was barely enough time for one celebration, it was left up to each person to come or not. The place was chosen for the event.

"They've got to eat," said the mayor.

There was a lot of fuss about where the picnic would be. Since I was the one who got the telegram, Lily had her say. "Joe Louis is our champion, and we ain't givin' him over."

The decision was made to have it at Jesse's church. There was lots of room, and a level playing field, just in case the Brown Bombers decided to play.

Church ladies all over town planned the menu, and food was the most important thing in the world. As far as food was concerned, there wasn't a pig, chicken, rabbit, pigeon, or frog safe in the area.

As plans progressed, it was decided that the train would be met at the station and Joe Louis would be given the key to the city. Following that, everybody would meet at the church grounds.

But as the big day drew near, I didn't hear anybody mentioning Champion.

"How come everybody's forgetting about him?" I asked. "Joe Louis is his hero; mine too, but not as much. We've got to get Champion back here. It's safe now!"

As usual, nobody paid me any mind.

Chapter Twenty-Two

O n the big day, a festive crowd gathered at the railroad depot. It was a beautiful day, not a cloud in the sky. Nobody knew what to expect, but they all wanted to be able to say they were there when it happened. Mr. Hopper had painted a banner that stretched across the front of the depot.

Welcome, Joe Louis,
World Heavyweight Champion,
and the Brown Bombers Softball Team!

Mayor Puckett stood on the platform with the key to the city to present to Mr. Louis. The high school band warmed up, and The Five Golden Stars Minus One got ready to sing. Lily was wearing her old hat trimmed with new pink silk roses. I kept thinking about Champion, and how he was gonna miss seeing the great man himself.

The train whistle blew one long and one short blast. Then Mr. Edwards brought engine number 1402 into the station, slick as glass. Billows of white steam floated out over the depot, enveloping the waiting crowd. The band played, the choir sang, and Lily's hat floated in clouds like a dream of roses.

When the steam cleared, Joe Louis smiled out at the crowd from the window of his special car. And standing next to him was Champion Always Luckey!

Lily let out a scream, and Lucius threw our hat up in the air.

"We wanted to surprise you," Mama said later. "But we had so many plans to work out to make it happen. At the same time, we were afraid something might go wrong."

I couldn't believe that Champion was back. On the way to the picnic, he told me everything. He talked so fast I could hardly keep up with him.

"I took the Greydog from Detroit to Atlanta," he said, "and Mr. Edwards met me and took me to Mr. Louis's special train at the station. I was so sleepy I thought I must be dreamin', but I wasn't, and that's how I got to meet Mr. Louis!" When he finally took a breath he said, "I been wantin' to come back."

* * *

Depression or not, folks knew how to put the little pot in the big pot and come up with good things to eat. Chicken and ribs were barbequed on oil drums cut in half. Platters were piled high with batter-fried frogs' legs, fried chicken,

144

stewed rabbit, and pigeon pie. An entire table was filled with desserts.

Jesse asked the blessing and the picnic was underway. Seated at the head table were Mr. Louis, Mayor Puckett, Mr. Edwards, two preachers, and some businessmen including Mr. Tamplin from the hardware store. The ballplayers were scattered among the crowd, so everybody could meet them.

Champion and I filled our plates and found a spot in the shade of a sycamore tree where we could watch everything.

"I can't believe you rode the train with Joe Louis!" I said. "Heck, I can't even ride on a train. And I couldn't get close to him because of the crowds."

"Don't worry," he said. "I already told him about you."

"What'd you tell him?" I was worried that he might've said how bad I was at sports.

"I told him you were my best friend," he said.

We got second helpings of fried chicken and started in eating again.

"A lot of chickens died for this picnic," said Champion.

"It's worth it," I said.

"I guess," he said, licking his fingers. "But you ain't a chicken."

I looked over at the head table. When Joe Louis first arrived, he was wearing a gray suit and a Panama straw hat. Now he sat hatless and coatless, trying to eat, sign autographs, and talk to a bunch of people, all at the same time. To add insult to injury, Swan was sitting next to him, chattering away.

"She makes me sick," I said. "Swan don't even like boxing.

I had to explain to her who Joe Louis is; she's just showing off."

* * *

As the afternoon wore on, patchwork quilts were spread under shade trees. Babies napped and ladies sat around in clusters, their paper fans going a mile a minute. Several games of horseshoes were in progress; the *clink, clink, clink* of metal against metal mixed with the sound of easy laughter. We decided to walk down to the pond.

Hard Labor Creek springs up in the hills, rushes through the woods, and goes back underground. Then it comes up in a clear stream that fills the pond behind Jesse's church. That's where he baptizes sinners. He's got a baptism stick to measure how deep the water is and where the holes are. When he's saving sinners, he doesn't want to lose them.

Willow trees leaned low over the still water. Dragonflies, blue as bottle glass, skimmed over the pond's surface. We took off our shoes and socks, and Champion rolled his trouser legs to his knees.

"My feet are hot," he said. "I'm goin' wading."

"You need your grandpa's baptism stick, so you won't step in a hole."

While he waded out into the pond, I stayed behind watching a school of tadpoles at the water's edge. They'd be frogs in no time; their tiny legs were already sprouting. I wished I'd brought a jar with me so I could take some home. Maybe Mama would let me make a pond in the garden.

The Everlasting Now

A wasp was buzzing around my head, and when I reached up to shoo him off, I looked over at Champion. My heart started pounding in my chest. A cottonmouth water moccasin was dangling from a pine branch directly over his head!

Sometimes water moccasins will drop down on you if you're in the water or in a boat. Not only could you die of snakebite, but you could be so scared you'd jump in the water and drown. Easy as I could, I walked toward Champion, keeping my eye on the snake the whole time. When I got closer, I called to him real soft-like.

"Champion," I said. He didn't hear me. "Champion," I said as loud as I dared.

He glanced over at me, and I pointed to the snake over his head. He looked up, thrashed about, lost his footing, and disappeared under the water.

Rushing over, I swam out to where he'd vanished. The water was barely up to my neck, but it was murky and dark. I was feeling for him under the water and tried to grab his shirt. But he began grabbing at me, nearly pulling me under. I was trying to hold on to him and keep my head above water, but I stepped in a hole and he slipped away from me.

When I got my head above water, I heard him coughing and sputtering, and I grabbed him again. "Don't fight me!" I said, putting my arm around his neck and pulling him into shallower water. We sloshed around a while until we could get our footing in the mud.

I half-dragged him onto the bank and we just lay there,

147

out of breath, muddy, and dripping wet. I looked over a little ways where I'd first seen the snake. He was gone. I took a deep breath.

The willow fronds parted with a sigh. Dusty and one of the ballplayers, whose name was Moe Majors, stepped out from the willow tree.

"Well, what in thunder?" said Dusty, coming over to us. "We were looking for you to have a game of catch. What happened?"

When Champion realized he had an audience, he sat up and said, "Brother saved my life! I was drowning and he saved me from a watery grave. I can't swim."

That scared me all over again.

"That was a brave thing you did, Brother," said Dusty.

"Sure was," said Moe Major.

Nobody ever called me brave before. "I was afraid, like always," I said. "I'm scared of snakes."

"Being brave doesn't mean you're not afraid," said Dusty. "It's when you do a thing in spite of being afraid that makes you brave."

After we'd dried off a little bit, we walked back up to the picnic.

"I hate to say it," said Dusty, "but you two look like drowned rats, and you're gonna have to face Lily and Miss Serena."

"I'm lucky to be alive," said Champion. "Aunt Lily ought to be happy."

"Me too," I said. Then I looked down at my clothes that were covered in mud.

"Let's see if we can get you boys a little help," said Moe.

The Everlasting Now

We kind of hung back at the edge of the picnic while he went to talk to Mr. Louis. A few minutes later, Mama and Lily came over to us acting real sweet. When they saw we were all right, they didn't say a thing about how we looked. I figured they were so thrilled to talk to the great man himself that they weren't too worried about our clothes being ruined.

After they left, Dusty brought us some lemonade and Mr. Louis stayed talking to us for a while. His voice surprised me. It wasn't deep, and he spoke real soft. I guess if you're a champion, you don't have to yell or holler.

"Did you always want to be a champion boxer?" I asked.

"No," he replied, "I just didn't want to be poor. And we were really poor when we lived here in Alabama. I didn't want my family to do without, so I did what I had to do. I've got a natural talent for boxing. It's a blessing and I'm grateful, but I have to work at it. Nobody's born a champion. Once you win doesn't mean you can quit trying, it just means you have to try harder."

* * *

At the end of the day, the food was packed up and the picnic tables emptied. Everyone scattered, getting their families together. Then, just about sunset, it was time to leave. There were animals to be fed, babies to be put to bed, and a train to catch. Nicodemus hauled a wagonload of folks to their homes. He wasn't mortgaged anymore; the debt on the mule had been paid.

I went over to the car where Mama and Swan were

waiting. As Swan climbed into the backseat, she whispered, "I'm glad you didn't drown, Brother."

Engine 1402 waited on the tracks, sighing softly. Steam rose like golden clouds in the setting sun. Then everybody who was supposed to boarded the train. Even Champion. Mr. Louis had arranged for his ticket to be left at Birmingham for his ride back to Detroit. I sure hated to see him go. At least he had on a clean shirt, Lily had seen to that. It looked like one of mine.

Champion called to me from the window. "Keep Joe Louis in a Bottle for me 'til I come back," he said.

Chapter Twenty-Three

Time passed faster than *The Joe Louis Special* steaming out of Snow Hill. Life was soon back to normal. School started. Miss Cubbage is my teacher this year. She's nice, not a bit like my last year's teacher whose spoiled rotten son used to sit in the back of the class eating candy and not offering anybody any.

There's a new girl in my class. Her name is Loretta Rivers. She has long blonde hair, and she smiled at me on the first day. Maybe school won't be so bad this year. I got glasses and can see better, but I hate them. You can bet your life Lamont Cranston doesn't wear glasses.

Every day after school, I picked up pecans 'til it grew too dark to find them in the rustling leaves. The tender smell of wood smoke hung on the air, and I could see the stars through the bare branches of the trees.

The grape arbor out back was filled with bronze-colored scuppernongs. That's the best smell in the world. I love scuppernongs better than muscadines, which are grapes too, only purple. Whichever kind I'm eating, I always pop the whole grape in my mouth and spit out the seeds. Swan's so persnickety she only eats the juicy pulp, spits out the seeds, and throws away the skins.

Lily baked scuppernong pies, then she and Mama made jelly and saved some for Mr. Holcomb. The last of the tomatoes were brought in and we ate fried green tomatoes that tasted almost as good as fried chicken.

* * *

My birthday's at the end of this month. I'll be twelve, the same age as the Maxwell. I'm not having a party 'cause I think that's sissy for boys. But our boarders will be here, and Lily's making my favorite caramel cake.

She had a letter from Rose who said that she has a new job. She is singing at The Chocolate Bar, a club owned by one of Mr. Louis's friends. I bet Champion had something to do with it. He probably talked a blue streak to Mr. Louis all the way to Birmingham. Rose said they're not as poor as they used to be, but she told Lily not to tell Jesse she was working at a nightclub.

On my actual birthday, Swan got up from the supper table, at a signal from Mama, and turned off the lights. Then Mama brought in the cake with the candles burning. Judge Tarzan darted under the sideboard, his eyes black as coal in the candlelight. "Black-eyed imp of Satan," is what Lily calls him. She likes him, but she said he's always underfoot, tripping her up.

The Everlasting Now

"Make a wish, Brother!" said Mama.

"And don't tell or it won't come true," said Swan.

Closing my eyes, I wished that I'd get to ride on a train before I got much older. Only I didn't think that telling or not telling would matter. It didn't look like it was about to happen anyway. I blew out the candles, everybody sang "Happy Birthday," and we cut the cake.

I got some good presents. Dusty gave me baseball cards and a Captain Marvel comic book. Captain Wooten brought me a fine harmonica. Champion sent a card that he had drawn, with a picture of Joe Louis that he'd cut out of the newspaper. Mr. Edwards gave me three Indian head pennies and a book called *She* by H. Rider Haggard, which he said was "a real adventure book."

"Try not to spend the pennies," he said. "One day they'll be worth a lot more than pennies." I put them in my cigar box that I keep under the bed.

* * *

The next evening, I sat with the men in the parlor listening to "The Railroad Hour" on the radio. Captain Wooten was playing solitaire, Dusty was resting his eyes, and Mr. Edwards was reading. The light from the floor lamp made a circle of gold around him. When the program was over, he motioned me over to the sofa and held out his book. It was the one with the essays he'd started reading from a while ago.

"This one's about riding in the cab of the engine of *The Twentieth Century Limited*," he said.

I'd looked at the picture of that train every day of my life, whenever I went to the kitchen or into the pantry. When Mr. Edwards began to read aloud, Captain Wooten stopped playing cards. Dusty opened his eyes and sat up straight in his chair.

> *This was not just air or earth that we flew upon,*
> *this was the seamless reality of Now...*
> *it was Time that we fed into the flaming furnace*
> *it was Time that flickered in the giant wheels.*
> *This was the everlasting Now.*

The words were like a place in a dream. Even though I wasn't sure what they meant, there was something inside them, like a promise. That night, I dreamed about my daddy. He was sitting in the club car of *The Twentieth Century Limited*, playing cards with Joe Louis.

* * *

The next morning, I met Mr. Edwards in the upstairs hall as he was coming out of his room. He was freshly shaven and smelled of bay rum hair tonic.

"What time do you have, Brother?"

"Mr. Edwards, you know I don't have a watch."

He took Jubilo from his pocket; the heavy gold watch and chain gleamed dully in the hall light.

"According to Jubilo, it's time for you to get ready," he said.

"Get ready for what?"

"For your real birthday present," he said. "We're taking you for a train ride. That is, if you want to go."

Had I heard him right? Had I? He was smiling to beat the band.

"Is it all right?" I asked.

"It surely is," he said.

This would be my very first train ride. I couldn't believe my birthday wish had come true! Of course I wanted to go, but I had to ask just one question. I sure didn't want to seem ungrateful, but there was something I had to know.

"Mr. Edwards, will I get to ride on the engine?"

"Right up in the cab," he said.

I nearly fell over myself going back to my room for my jacket.

Everything had been arranged. The rule not to allow civilians on the engine had been waived. I was going to ride in the cab of a Mikado engine all the way to Montgomery, Alabama, and back again!

Mama, Lily, and Swan came to see us off. The train was primed and ready to roll. Billows of steam curled around the depot rafters. The sharp smell of valve oil cut the air.

The engine throbbed and quivered, waiting to be set free. Standing next to her, I could feel the powerful vibrations of that mighty heart pulsing through the soles of my shoes.

"Welcome aboard, Brother," said Captain Wooten, giving me a boost up to the cab where Mr. Edwards and Dusty were waiting.

The cushions on the seat boxes were dark plush. Nickel-plated reverse levers, throttle, and lubricators gleamed. Flames flickered through the glass butterfly doors of the firebox. Dials shone white; their thin needles quivered. The inside of the cab looked like a clock shop, but I didn't see a clock. Time waits in the engineer's pocket.

Down the line, signal lights glowed like the hearts of emeralds.

"Green!" shouted Dusty above the noise of the engine.

"Green!" echoed Mr. Dupree from the platform.

He gave a wave and we were on our way! With a mighty roar, that magnificent machine divided the clear, autumn afternoon.

Dusty checked the gauges. He tapped the face on a dial with his finger.

"You got to keep the gauge at 220," he said. "No black smoke, and don't let the safety valve lift. Every time she lifts, that's twenty gallons of water wasted."

Light flashed on the rods, and flames danced in the firebox. The gauge was steady, and the old girl was talking in the language only railroaders understood.

Steam escaped from the cylinders in a rush; the blower lifted the smoke. I heard the pounding beat of the air pumps. *That's her breathing!* I thought. It was like a dream, only better than all my dreams of trains.

"Okay, Brother," said Mr. Edwards. "Take the whistle."

I blew the whistle in his signature—a long and a short that went wailing over the countryside. At that glorious sound, I felt like a part of the engine. My heart beat along with hers. I wanted to lay my hand on her, so she'd know how proud I was, how I felt about her.

Autumn fields and orchards rushed past. People waved from roadsides and villages as the train passed by on her journey. Leaning from the window, I watched the rest of the train following obediently behind us. I saw the flash of her great pistons. Time flickered in the giant wheels, in what Mr. Morley had called "the everlasting Now."

I was so happy I felt like my heart would burst. And I knew, I knew, there couldn't be anything better in the whole world than driving a steam engine on shining rails, across fields, through cities and small towns, and all across America.

The End

SARA HARRELL BANKS was raised in Georgia and Alabama by a number of loving and eccentric relatives. She comes from a newspaper family and has followed in the tradition of her great-grandfather, who was editor and publisher of the *Choctaw Herald,* and her grandmother, who was his printer's devil and wished to write stories for the paper.

A journalist and author, Ms. Banks has informed and entertained adults and children alike. Her books for children include *Remember My Name,* a novel for middle grade readers. She won the 1997 Georgia Author of the Year award for *Under the Shadow of Wings,* which was named an American Booksellers Pick of the Lists and hailed by *School Library Journal* as "powerful and compelling." She received the Georgia Author of the Year award in 2000 in the young adult division for *Abraham's Battle: A Novel of Gettysburg.*

She lives in High Point, North Carolina, with her middle aged cat Enoch, named for her father, who had changed his name. The tradition of eccentricity continues.